KISS ME AGAIN

HOLIDAY HEARTS

SUSAN SCOTT SHELLEY

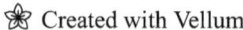

CHAPTER ONE

Kira Kallis glared at the emails of Valentine's Day themed ads in her inbox. Two weeks until the holiday and reminders were everywhere. Hearts in countless shades of red and pink, bouquets of flowers, boxes of chocolates, and chubby cupids all taunted her from store windows, grocery lines, TV commercials, and email blasts.

One by one, they ended up in her trash folder.

Being alone hadn't bothered her last year. But this year, she'd turned thirty, and nearly all of her friends were married or matched up. After months of being the third or fifth wheel, she'd felt truly alone.

Why was finding someone so hard?

With a quick glance toward her open office door, she logged onto the online dating site she'd joined. The outer floor slowly stirred awake as more members of the sales and marketing departments arrived. Snow and icy roads reduced her crew to a skeleton staff. Snippets of conversations about upcoming weekend plans and complaints about the weather drifted toward her as employees clad in Casual Friday attire strode by. She'd have a few extra minutes to see if her latest match had responded to her email before someone needed her attention.

And that was the problem. Everyone needed her attention and she'd given away too much of herself. She'd dedicated years working her way up to her position as marketing director at her family's toy company. She loved her job, even though her long hours had been the reason her last two relationships had ended.

The site loaded more slowly than usual. She tapped her mouse against the desk as she waited. Her personal page followed the guidelines on crafting an eye-catching profile—listed her hobbies, interests, fun facts, and flattering photos. She'd received a fair share of "interested" responses, but date after date, that spark of connection had eluded her.

But her latest match had the potential to be The One.

The site loaded. No new messages.

Great. At this rate, meeting someone she could spend Valentine's Day with wasn't going to happen.

The hollowness in her gut hurt. She rolled her chair away from her desk and crossed to the window. Snow covered the trees, falling at a quick pace, blanketing the ground faster than the plows could clear the parking lot. Inhaling deep breaths and watching the peaceful scene helped eased the ache.

"Hey, kid. Glad you made it in okay." Her brother's voice jarred her out of her concentration. No matter that he was only five years older than she. He'd called her *kid* from the time she'd been one, but had the good graces not to do it at the office.

"Damon, please…" She rolled her eyes and turned. Her retort died on her lips.

Next to Damon stood his best friend and the company's hotshot IT guy, Hunter York.

In contrast to her dark haired, dark eyed brother, Hunter had dark blond hair and blue eyes. And the best smile in Holiday, New York. Heck, in all of Western New York. Dark jeans and a black sweater with sleeves pushed up showcased his tall, muscular frame. His eyes crinkled at the corners with his smile. "There's bagels, donuts, fruit, and coffee in the break room. Everyone's grabbing their share now. Want to join us?"

"I could use more coffee. Give me a minute. I need to finish up something first."

"Is it the report I sent you for the projected first quarter sales? There was a glitch in the spreadsheet. Here, I'll show you." Damon strode toward her desk.

And the dating site was in full view. He was going to flip out. She hurried to beat him to her computer. "Wait! Don't touch it. I have a few programs running."

They reached the desk at the same time. Clicked Hearts' site, with its bright blue background and hot pink valentines, lit up her screen like a screaming advertisement of her loneliness.

Damon's gaze whipped from the screen to her face.

"What the hell is this? You're not actually *on* that dating site, are you?"

Her cheeks heated. "So what if I am?"

Desperately, she shook the mouse and rolled it over her desk, but the arrow didn't respond. Wishing she was on her laptop instead of the desktop computer wouldn't help her now. She couldn't close out of the site or minimize the screen. She couldn't do anything except pray the floor would open up and swallow her. "Damn it, the screen's frozen."

"Let me have a look." Hunter squeezed between her and the desk, leaving her no choice but to take a step back. She stood to his right, watching as his fingers tapped at keys. His gaze narrowed on her dating profile. "Brown Eyed Girl?"

The rush of heat crept up to her ears. More than a little aware of Hunter's closeness, she crossed her arms over her chest and tried to ignore the tingle when his shoulder brushed hers. "Everyone needs a user name. It was the first thing that came to mind."

Damon leaned on her desk, hands closed into fists, shaking his head. "What are you doing? Online dating? You don't know these guys."

"It's no different than meeting someone in a bar or at work, or anywhere else."

"At least you can physically see who you're talking to in those situations. You can make some sort of judgment. Online is a license to be fake."

Kira shrugged, entirely uncomfortable to have the

conversation at all, but especially in front of Hunter. "Being able to see someone's face doesn't show anything about what they're like on the inside."

Damon stiffened, and regret struck her in the chest. He'd met his ex, Ursula, in a bar. She'd lied, a lot, and had left him without a word, taking off with half the contents of his apartment and his bank account. Trying to track her down and reclaim his property was sucking up huge chunks of his time. He'd been running on empty for weeks.

"Don't worry. I'll be fine. I'm careful." She forced a smile, but he didn't seem convinced, staring at her with a mixture of exhaustion, exasperation, and concern.

Hunter straightened to full height. At six-foot-two, he was a good nine inches taller than she was. He grinned down at her. "There. You're fixed, Brown Eyed Girl, but you'll have to log back into the system. And your Clicked Hearts."

When she looked into his eyes, her heartbeat quickened—fast beats keeping time with the flutter in her stomach. And as always, she pretended they didn't exist. He was her friend and had never given any indication that the attraction she felt was more than one-sided. "Thanks."

"Anytime." He turned to Damon. "Why don't we let Kira get back to what she was doing and grab some food? Aidan's waiting for us."

The mention of the friend who made up the remaining member of the guys' tight trio finally made

Damon move toward the door. "Be careful, kid. We'll talk about this later."

She nodded her thanks for the reprieve, then closed the door and locked it behind them.

The last thing she needed was her brother involved in her dating life.

Hunter led Damon out of Kira's office. Had he been alone, he'd have found a reason to stay and talk with her. Poor Kira. She looked so flustered by her brother.

Lips pinched, Damon shook his head as they walked. He shoved his hand through his hair. Worry grooves formed on his forehead. "I don't like it. I didn't know she was on that site. Anyone could be on the other side of that screen. What if it's some sicko who wants to hurt her—or worse? Or the same thing that happened to me happens to her? There are too many stories out there of things that could go wrong."

Hunter grunted in agreement. Annoyance pricked along his skin, and his hands formed fists. The idea of something happening to Kira twisted his gut. Beautiful, sexy, smart, and caring, she mattered, more than was wise. "I know you're still sorting out a lot of stuff from Ursula. I'll keep an eye on Kira for you. You don't have to worry about her."

"Thanks, bro." Damon let out a heavy breath, his anguish obviously abated. "I know I can always count on you."

Ever since boot camp, he and Damon and Aidan had always had each other's backs. They'd served together. Fought together.

Hunter tucked his hands into his pockets and felt through the material for the dimples where the first bullets had sliced him. The four identical scars on his legs were a constant reminder of the day of the ambush. He'd laid on the ground, bleeding out and unable to walk, while Damon had covered him from enemy fire, protecting him until the threat had ceased, and then had dragged him to safety.

Throughout coffee and breakfast in the break room with his buddies, his thoughts drifted to his slow and painful rehab, when he'd been discharged and returned home to LA, unsure what to do with his life, drinking to deal with the memories and the lingering pain rehab and surgery could never cure. Damon had pulled him out of that downward spiral, too, moving him clear across the country and giving him a job at his family's company.

Someday, he would find a way to repay his friend. Helping ease Damon's mind over Kira was the least he could do.

He left Damon in the break room with Aidan. After filling two paper cups with coffee—black for him and with two splashes of peppermint creamer for Kira—he trekked back to her office. When she opened the door, a faint blush still stained her cheeks. He handed her a coffee. "Here."

"Thanks." She raised the cup and inhaled. "Peppermint. This day just got better. I think I can make it through now. You're the best."

Her words tugged out his smile. She'd been taking her coffee the same way every day for years. He paid attention. "Got a minute?"

"Sure." Brown eyes wide, she ushered him in. "What's up?"

He nodded toward the computer. "I thought we could talk about the dating site."

Even through the tailored white shirt and tan sweater she wore, he could see her stiffen. She tossed her long sun-kissed brown hair over her shoulder and then nailed him with her best *no-nonsense* look and her chin jutting out. "Why? Do you want to create a profile?"

"No." He sipped the dark brew, hoping the scent of coffee would cover up the inviting mix of vanilla and flowers of her perfume. It messed with his head every time he smelled it. It made him want things he shouldn't. "Damon is worried about you."

The slope of her shoulders softened. "I know he is. I wish he wouldn't. I'm not an idiot."

"He doesn't think you're an idiot. Neither do I. I've seen you almost every day for four years. You wouldn't be in that chair if you weren't incredibly smart and sharp as a sniper. But his concern is legitimate."

"When my brother gets stuck on something, he really digs in." She waved her hand over her desk. "Grab a seat and have a look at the site. Then you can tell him everything is okay."

He pulled one of her guest chairs around to join her.

Hot pink hearts highlighted an electric blue screen. "Do you need sunglasses when you're on here?"

"Ugh. It's so glaring. If I ran their account, the first thing I'd do is tone down the hues." A smile bloomed across her face, and his heartbeat stuttered. God, she was beautiful.

He forced his attention back to the screen and leaned closer. An open chat window between Kira and some guy who called himself... "Seriously? His handle is Real Life Romeo?"

She shrugged. "It's cheesy but better than some of the names I've come across. I prefer Romeo over crude references to anatomy."

"I like *your* handle. Brown Eyed Girl is cute." He leaned against the chair's back. "So how long have you been talking to Romeo here?"

"His real name is Byron. We've been chatting for a few weeks. He likes a lot of the same things I do—running, yoga, charity work, and animals."

The guy's picture was darkened, half in shadows. Artistic but not great for a clear view. "Has he asked to meet you yet?"

"No, but I don't immediately go out with these guys. I talk to them for a little bit first and try to get to know them." Her gaze narrowed. "I'm thirty, not fifteen. I'm not going to be careless with my safety or the information I share."

"How many guys are you talking to or seeing right now?"

She blinked at him over her cup. With a sigh, she set

it on her desk. "I've been on the site for a couple of months. I'm not seeing anyone right now. The last few guys fizzled out after the first date and the only guy I'm talking to now is Byron. Why?"

"Just curious. You haven't mentioned this online dating during any of our morning runs with the group or any other time we hang out outside of work." During morning runs, he'd hang back with Kira while Damon and Aidan took the lead. Occasionally, some buddies from their hockey team would join them. The mornings spent with her were the highlights of his week.

Pink spots appeared on her cheeks, and she shifted in her chair. "It's not easy for me to talk about. I'm tired of being alone, so I'm trying to do something to actively change that."

He resisted the urge to wrap his arms around her and pull her into his lap and claim her as his. He didn't like the idea of her trying to find someone else, but she deserved someone whole—not damaged goods—and he qualified as definitely damaged. "You go after what you want. That's brave. But if this guy has been talking to you for a month on a dating site and isn't trying to schedule a time to see you in person, that doesn't seem to add up right."

She opened her mouth, but he lifted his hand to cut off her argument. He was pretty damn good at research. He could help her. "Let me check into him."

"How?"

"You have how many photos of yourself on your profile?"

"Five. The site suggests that you show yourself doing activities you enjoy." She clicked on each of her photos. One of her in her running gear. One of her volunteering at a Veteran's Day event held the prior year. Another of her in yoga attire, sitting in lotus position. One of her taken at the company's annual kids' Christmas party. And her main profile picture—her laughing into the camera, eyes bright, lips shiny—she radiated a glow.

By contrast, Romeo's photos seemed muted and dull. Hunter leaned over her and dragged one of his profile pictures into the search engine. "Let's see what comes up. Maybe he also uses this for one of his social media profiles."

The search only yielded the dating site in the results.

Hunter frowned at the image. "You like this guy a lot?"

She tilted her head to the side for a moment. "We seem to have a lot in common."

"According to the blue dot on his page, he was active within the last few minutes. Message him now and ask him to meet you."

Shifting in her seat, she pushed her hair over her shoulder and treated him to a whiff of vanilla. "Well... I guess I know him well enough."

"Do it. I want to see what we're dealing with." Hunter paused to grab his coffee and give his brain a chance to settle. "Tell him to meet you in a public place."

Her brow arched and she leveled him with a look

before turning her attention to the screen. Her fingers flew over the keyboard. "Not an idiot, remember? I've always met them in public places. Snowflake Skates has their outdoor skating rink open until the end of the month. That would be a good spot."

Hunter watched the screen as the chat bubble appeared.

Brown-Eyed-Girl: Are you free this weekend? I thought we could meet for real.

She blew out a breath. "Done."

"Good job." He toasted her with his coffee.

Real-Life-Romeo: Live and in person? Not sure I'm ready to bring the mystery to an end...

Hunter straightened and set his coffee down with a thud. "That's his response? He's joking, right?"

Kira shrugged. "It's hard to tell tone in email and texts. Maybe he's kidding."

Brown-Eyed-Girl: Maybe we could go ice skating.

After a full two minutes had passed without a response, she twisted toward him. Pink crept up her neck. "You don't have to stay for this. I'll let you know what happens."

He pulled his phone from his pocket. "I don't mind hanging around. I have a few system checks to do."

Kira minimized the dating site and brought up the spreadsheet she and Damon had discussed earlier. "Are you hacking into the company servers again?"

"Every Friday. It keeps my team fresh."

"It drives them crazy." She smiled, and then laughed when he feigned surprise. "I overheard some gossip in the break room. But I think they really like the challenge."

They worked silently, side by side, until Kira's soft fingers latched onto his forearm. "He just agreed. We're meeting on Sunday afternoon. Two o'clock, at the skating rink."

"Good. I'll be close by." He set his phone aside, mind made up, prepared for her argument.

Her fingers loosened but didn't let go, and her smile faded to a frown. "You can't come on my date."

"You don't know this guy. And I think it's weird he didn't ask to meet you sooner."

She leaned away from the computer and sighed. "No one observed me when I went on the other dates, and I was fine. Knowing where I'm going to meet him should be enough."

"You weren't fine. You were lucky."

"Not lucky. Careful. I send all the date information to my friend Emily. Phone numbers. Meeting place. I even text her when I get home. Since she's traveling and Damon's being so overprotective, I'll just send that info to him or you."

Kira was strong, but something about the guy irked him. "Great if you go missing. I want to prevent that." When her lips pursed, he moved in closer and lowered his voice. "Would you like Damon there instead?"

"No," she said quickly. Her frown morphed into wide eyes and raised eyebrows. "He'd probably copy the guy's plate and call in favors from the cops."

"I'm a pro at watching from the shadows." Unable

to help himself, he brushed his fingers over the back of her hand. Silky smooth, the contact ignited a need for more. He dropped his hand to his side. "You won't even see me."

She hesitated for a second, then met his gaze. "Fine. You're hired."

CHAPTER TWO

The outdoor skating rink was the perfect place to spend a winter afternoon. Kira stood by the admission counter, smiling at the families and couples and groups of people that passed. The sun shined bright in a cloudless sky, and the cold air wasn't bone-chilling. Great weather for skating, if she ever got to the skating part.

Twenty minutes past their arranged time, and Byron hadn't yet called or texted or sent any message through the dating site. Her excitement over finally meeting him dwindled. Lateness was one of her pet peeves. She sent him a text to check in and then shifted the bag holding her skates to her other shoulder.

Five minutes later, her phone remained silent. The lone text she'd received had been from Hunter when he'd arrived at one-thirty. True to his promise, she couldn't see him anywhere.

She waited five more minutes, until two-thirty, and then called the number Byron had given her. When his voicemail picked up, she left a message telling him she'd only wait a few more minutes before leaving.

Her phone pinged with a text alert.

Finally.

But Hunter's name appeared across her screen, not Byron's.

Hunter: Any word from Romeo? He's really late...

Thirty minutes was enough time wasted. She typed her reply.

Kira: No word from him, and no responses to my call or texts. I'm done waiting. Where are you?

Rather than a response, he emerged from behind the first aid tent and approached her. So tall, in dark jeans, a dark jacket, and a navy watch cap, he commanded attention. "Sorry he didn't show."

Trying to battle back the hurt and embarrassment, she shrugged. Dealing with being stood up on her own was one thing, dealing with it under Hunter's scrutiny was another. Pretending to be unaffected required effort but she managed a smile. "Thanks for coming. I guess I'll see you in the morning for our run."

"Hold on." His gloved hand touched her elbow, and she felt the contact all the way through her coat and sweater like skin on skin. "You came here to skate, so we should skate."

"You want to stay?"

His cheeks creased into a smile and a spark of light shined in his dark blue gaze. "I had to skip my hockey game yesterday, so I need the workout. Let's go."

She wasn't the kind of girl to wait at home for a guy

to call. No way would she sit around moping because Byron hadn't shown up. And Hunter never failed to make her smile. "All right. I hate to miss out on a chance to get on the ice."

After a stop at his car to grab his hockey skates, they joined the line of people waiting at the admission counter. Hunter's tall presence by her side shielded her from the cold wind whipping across the open field. He stepped in closer to allow a group of kids to pass, and a hint of citrus and spice wafted over her.

That scent. His scent. It both reassured her and stirred her blood. If only the guys she met on Clicked Hearts were like Hunter. If only he'd look at her like he thought of her as anything more than an honorary sister...

When they reached the front of the line, he leaned over her, cash in hand. "Two. We don't need skate rentals."

She twisted toward him. "You don't have to pay for me."

"You can get the hot chocolates later." He winked. And then guided her toward a bench. The area wasn't crowded, but he sat close to her anyway.

They laced up their skates and stowed their bags and shoes in a locker. He kept his hand on her back as they walked to the rink on blades. Almost like a date.

When they reached the rink, an attendant opened the door in the boards to let them onto the ice. Hunter turned to her, palm up, arm extended. "Ready?"

She slid her hand into his strong, secure grip. Their

hands fit together perfectly. She blushed heat against the cold and followed him onto the smooth as glass surface.

Once they began skating and gained speed, he let go. She thought he would have skated ahead. Instead, they glided around the rink side by side. The music blaring from the speakers and Hunter by her side soothed her spirit, and she realized she wasn't all that disappointed that Byron had bailed.

For as much time as she spent with Hunter—the morning runs, time at the office, dinners with her brother and Aidan—she never tired of him. Even now, he made her laugh, challenging her to silly skating contests. After two speed races they'd deemed a draw, she took off, executing a triple salchow at center ice. Cold wind whipped around her, tossing her hair into her face. Laughing, she shook it back and scanned the ice for Hunter.

He skated to a stop by her side. "Nice moves."

"It's been more than ten years since I took lessons. I'm a little rusty. But every time I skate, I have to try it. I bet I could teach you."

"Teach me to do that? I doubt it." He grinned down at her. They turned in a circle, keeping pace, mirroring each other's movements.

A man skated up to them. "Hey, York. I thought that was you."

Hunter's smile fell away and his features hardened into a stony glare. "Waverly."

Waverly shot Kira a sly leer that made her skin crawl and then he turned back to Hunter. "Your girlfriend has some pretty good moves. You should put her on your team. Break out a few of those fancy spins and at least you'd be entertaining. But you don't stand a chance of winning."

Hunter shifted in front of Kira, placing himself between her and the smaller man. "Get lost, man. And watch your back. I'll be gunning for you."

"Bring it on." With a smirk, Waverly skated away.

Hunter's glare tracked the guy as he moved into the crowd. All traces of fun had fled his face. The mood shifted, too. Tension poured off of him.

Kira touched his arm, but he continued to watch the other man. "Waverly's on the Dragons, isn't he? Damon has mentioned his name before. He's not a fan."

"Waverly's teammates are his only fans. No one else in the league likes him. He takes too many cheap shots." As he spoke, he rubbed the outside of his thigh.

Was he remembering a cheap shot, or was he in genuine pain? "We can leave if his being here is going to bother you."

Hunter's head snapped in her direction. The twin flames of anger in his eyes faded. "I'm fine."

But his hand remained on his leg, and she caught his slight wince. He needed a break and was too stubborn to take one.

She admired him for his bravery and his service to his country. Her heart ached over the injuries he'd sustained and the pain he still endured. Not that he'd talk about the pain. In the four years they'd known each other, she'd learned he kept that part closed off, and he hated any attention drawn to what he considered a weakness. But she'd also learned the signs to look for, tells that he probably wasn't aware he had.

If he wouldn't let her help him, then she'd work around his pride. "I'm pretty thirsty. Would you mind if we headed to the snack bar?"

The tension in his features relaxed. "Let's go."

When they reached the snack area, she asked him to grab a table, then headed off for the hot chocolate line. He sat facing away from the concessions, legs kicked out, massaging his thigh. If he thought the table would allow him to be discrete, he was mistaken. His position didn't hide the grimace twisting his face or the brooding expression that followed.

Her heart hurt for him. She wished he'd let her in. She wound her way back to their table and placed the cups steaming with decadent cocoa sweetness in front of him with a flourish. "Here you go. They even gave us extra marshmallows."

His hand stopped moving and the shadows darkening his face eased. Blue eyes warmed with his smile and only a hint of his guard remained. "Thanks."

She might not be able to take away Hunter's pain, but she could shift his attention away from it. Determined to make him laugh, she scooted her chair closer to his and pointed out some of the other skaters' on-ice antics. His laughter was as rich as the cocoa and much sweeter.

For the first time all afternoon, she was glad Byron had flaked on their date.

Hunter hadn't corrected Waverly's assumption that she was his girlfriend. Even though she wasn't, she *was* his friend. Maybe this extra time they were spending together would allow him to open up more, to admit when he was hurting and allow her to be there for him. And she *wanted* to be there for him.

Knowing she was helping him right now felt good. Whether he wanted to admit it or not, Hunter needed her.

Hunter moved closer to Kira as a new group of people barreled onto the ice. They'd been skating for well over an hour since their last stop for snacks. His legs ached, but he didn't want to ruin the afternoon for her by suggesting they go home. "You look cold. Want another hot chocolate?"

"I don't know of any woman who'd turn down chocolate." Smiling up at him, she linked their arms. "Let's go."

In her white pea coat, white knit hat and white scarf, she looked like a snow angel. And angel was right. She'd been the only thing keeping him from knocking out Waverly. The jerk circled the ice at the opposite end of the rink. He needed to pay for trying to take Damon out at the knees during the last game they played. Hunter couldn't wait for the rematch.

Hot chocolate in hand, they wandered past the benches facing the rink and over to the seats surrounding the fit pit. Braced against the stinging pain in his thighs, he lowered himself onto the seat. Sometimes, the pain felt like tiny fires. Sometimes, an annoying ache. Other times, the tingling was enough to drive him crazy.

But at least he'd come home in one piece. Other soldiers weren't so lucky. He'd suck up his problems as best he could, and shoulder them alone.

As flames danced high, Kira sat beside him. "When do you guys have games this week?"

"Tomorrow night and Wednesday."

"Since we skated today and you're playing tomorrow night, are you still going for a run with the guys tomorrow morning?"

He would, as long as his body didn't rebel completely. Cold weather affected him—specifically his legs—more than he liked to admit. "We have a run scheduled, I'm going to be there for it."

"Okay. If you won't slack off, I guess I can't either." With a smile, she nudged his shoulder. She never slacked off on the running group. Every time, she was right there waiting for him, and she filled their runs with happy conversation that distracted him from his pain.

If things were different, if she weren't the sister of one of his best friends, if he weren't riddled with pain, if she weren't trying to find someone else, then he'd let himself imagine how easy it would be to stay in bed with her and skip the outside workout. They'd create their own exercise while tangled in his sheets. He had a feeling she'd fit perfectly against him. Hot, sweaty, energetic sex. Slow, sweet, lazy sex. Sliding against each other, skin to skin, with nothing between them at all.

His body hardened at the images, and he directed his thoughts away from that dangerous thread. "What are you going to do about Byron?"

Her smile faded, and she lifted her delicate shoulders in a shrug. "I guess I'll just see what happens. I'm going to wait to hear from him."

"If he apologizes, will you see him again?"

"I guess so. But there had better be a damn good reason for standing me up."

"Being eaten by a bear is a good reason. Saying he forgot is a ridiculous one."

Her laugh tumbled out. "Being eaten by a bear isn't a ridiculous reason?"

"Nope. Neither is saving the world if you're a superhero. Or wrestling with an alligator. Ridiculous to me is something that shows you don't matter enough for someone to try to be there—like blowing off plans at the last minute, or showing up late, or not calling at all."

They spent the next several minutes debating good reasons and dreaming up ridiculous ones. He loved that he could be himself with her, and he wasn't quite ready for their time together to come to an end. "Do you want to skate again?"

She stood and stretched. "Sure. Maybe just a few more times around the rink? But nothing fancy and no contests this time."

"You got it." The heat from the fire pit had helped

his legs. He stood, and tossed their cups into the trash and then turned toward the ice. She caught up with him and linked her arm through his again. He liked the idea of her holding onto him—a little too much. Creating distance would be smart, but for now, he'd let himself pretend he could have her.

A few more times around the rink turned into another hour, then a stop for pizza at the sports bar on the drive home. They shared a half veggie, half pepperoni pie and watched the first period of the Buffalo-Toronto hockey game. Kira sat next to him, rather than opposite him. He was surprised by the move. Pleased, but surprised. He draped his arm across the back of the booth and sat as close to her as he dared—closer than he'd be if Damon or Aidan were around.

She just made him happy. Maybe he was a selfish guy, but he wanted that happiness, wanted it bottled up and stored in his soul, filed away for days when the pain got too bad. He'd remember how her face lighted up and how she smiled at him, close enough to touch, and it would help him get through.

She pushed the last slice in his direction. "I can't believe I ate as much as I did. This one is all yours."

"Skating for hours builds up an appetite." He picked off a piece of pepperoni and brought it up to her mouth. Her eyes widened, but she parted her lips. He slipped the bite inside and held back a groan at the way her eyes darkened when his thumb brushed her lower lip.

Desire clawed through him, tempting him to repeat

the touch, to feel her lips against his skin, any part of his skin.

The patrons in the booths around them erupted into a cheer at the action on the TV screens. The noise reminded him that they weren't alone. Hunter twisted to see the Buffalo players gathered on the ice celebrating a goal. Pain shifted from stinging to stabbing on the side of his thigh. Muffling a curse, he pressed his hand to his leg.

Kira touched his arm. He felt the contact all the way to his fingers. Her gaze was on his thigh and his hand, sympathy in her eyes.

Desired cooled, burned away by white hot fury at his injuries and the fact that the nerve pain never went the fuck away. With stiff movements, he shifted away from her touch. He grabbed his drink with his other hand and squeezed the cold glass. "Great goal. Did you see that replay?"

"Hunter..." Her gaze jumped from his eyes to his thigh, then back again. "Are you okay? Can I help—"

"I'm fine." Frustration tightening his lips, he snapped out the words. Talking about pain, about his weakness, wasn't happening. Not with her. Not with anyone.

Her chest puffed up like she was about to say something but then she pressed her lips together and picked up her drink and faced the TV.

They watched the rest of the period in awkward silence. He kept his focus on the large screen, but memories of the day of the attack, then of his time in the hospital and rehabbing his body, and then of the dark days he'd spent drinking, played through his mind like a morbid highlight reel.

When the buzzer sounded, ending the game, Kira slid her empty glass to the center of the table. Eyes cast down, she slipped from the booth. "We should go."

The move snapped him from his memories, and the hurt he saw in her features stabbed him in the gut. Hunter pushed to his feet, gritting his teeth against the tingling radiating down his thigh. Kira shrugged into her coat. Before she could move more than a step away, he clasped her shoulder and turned her to face him. "I'm sorry I snapped at you earlier."

Biting her lip, she nodded and then her lips curved into a gentle smile. "It's fine."

He didn't deserve her easy forgiveness. Before he could say anything further, she linked her arm through his and turned toward the exit. They weren't skating or teetering through the arena on thin blades. There wasn't any reason for them to hold on to each other, but he couldn't make himself pull away again. The pain slowed his pace. Kira had to notice; her steps slowed to match his, but she didn't say anything about his weakness. Instead, she made remarks about the game and about the cold air that slapped their skin when they exited the warmth of the bar.

After a short drive, Hunter pulled into Kira's driveway, he was exhausted and aching, but happy he'd had her to himself for the bulk of the day.

She unbuckled her seatbelt and turned to him.

"Thank you for today. I know I was initially against your spying, but I'm really happy you were there. I," she hesitated, "I ended up having an amazing time."

"It was fun." That was an understatement, but he couldn't let on how much he'd enjoyed being with her.

"Thanks to you." Leaning toward him, she opened her arms and wrapped them around him.

He reached to return the hug and the damn seatbelt cut into his neck. His right hand released the belt's lock and, free, he wrapped his arms around her body. Nose in her hair, he breathed her in. Kira smelled so damn sexy. When she moved to pull away, he kept her in place with a hand on the middle of her back, needing just a little more time.

For a long moment, they watched each other, then he gave into need and cupped her cheek with his hand. "Kira."

Her hands gripped his back. Dark eyes focused on his mouth, and her own lips parted. When her gaze lifted to his, his thoughts scrambled. He forgot about all the reasons why kissing her was a bad idea.

Her tongue peeked out to wet her lips.

Body pulsing with the desire to taste her, he leaned in.

His phone buzzed, and the tune he'd selected for Damon and Aidan rang out, as effective as dousing him with a bucket of cold water. Remembering who he was, he retreated and eased back. "I should go."

Kira nodded and withdrew. "Right, right. Well, I'll

see you in the morning. For the run. And work. Right. Good night."

She grabbed her skate bag and rushed out of the car.

He waited until she went inside, then he checked his phone.

Damon had called.

He should be thankful that the phone call had kept him from making a huge mistake. But now that he'd nearly had a taste of Kira, he didn't think he'd be able to shake that from his mind.

CHAPTER THREE

On Monday morning, Kira walked into the conference room with her notes for her part of the staff meeting tucked against her chest. Hunter stood at the front of the room, setting up equipment and fixing someone's slide show presentation.

He'd been quiet during their run and had kept to himself. They'd been part of a larger group, with more of the hockey team joining them, and that hadn't allowed any time for private conversation. She'd thought about their near-kiss constantly—how he'd looked, how his lips had parted, and how his eyes seemed to see into her soul. What would have happened if that phone call hadn't interrupted them? What did it mean? And the big question—what happened now?

She greeted several coworkers as she made her way to the front of the room. When Hunter raised his head and met her gaze, she smiled and received a nod and half-smile in reply. Heart lighter, she walked toward him.

Grant Parsons from the Accounting Department strolled to her side, grinning. "Hey, Kira. How was your date?"

He'd been the one to tell her about Clicked Hearts. From the stories he shared with her before every Monday's staff meeting, he was having a much better run of luck with his matches.

He hadn't lowered his voice. She bristled as ten pairs of eyes turned in their direction. With a smile plastered on her face, she bent her head over her notes and kept her voice low. "Let's just say it didn't go as planned. He stood me up."

"His loss. He doesn't know what he's missing." He laid his hand on her shoulder for a moment. Concern filled his dark gaze. "You okay? You could have called me after it happened. You can call me anytime."

His response surprised her. He'd been with the company a year and had asked her out soon after being hired. After one date, they'd both decided they were better off as friends, but friendly co-workers was a better description of their relationship. They never met up or chatted outside of work.

"Thanks, but I ended up hanging out with a friend, so it worked out okay."

Hunter's scent, that spicy citrus cologne, wafted from behind her. Relief as soft as a ribbon and awareness as sharp as a blade fought for dominance. She twisted toward him. His fingertips barely grazed the small of her back. "Everything's all set up."

She searched his gaze, but Grant hovered too close, not allowing them any privacy. "Thanks. I guess it's time to get started."

Hunter leveled Grant with a hostile look, and then his features softened when he focused back on her. "Call me if you need me."

She nodded, but before she could say anything else, he left.

The meeting and then another swallowed up her morning. Kira didn't get back to her office until lunchtime and found Byron's message waiting for her in the chat box.

Real-Life-Romeo: So sorry I missed our date. I pulled an all-nighter with a work emergency and slept through the alarm I'd set. I'll make it up to you.

A work emergency? She could believe that. But why wait so long to text her? She doubted that he'd slept for a full twenty-four hours straight.

She wanted to call Hunter. But should she? He'd said he'd wanted to know when she heard from her no-show date. After debating for a few minutes, she sent him a text with Byron's reason.

He responded immediately.

Hunter: No way. If you could see me, I'm scoffing at his excuse.

The awkwardness she'd felt disappeared at his fast, easy response. Grinning, she typed out, *And how exactly does one look when scoffing?*

She didn't have to wait long for his reply.

Hunter: I'm in the exec suite fixing your dad's computer. I'll swipe some of the good coffee and bring it down when I'm done. Then I'll scoff in person.

She smiled to herself, then realized he was acting as he'd had pre-skate. Maybe they didn't have to talk about what had happened the night before, after all. Maybe it hadn't happened as she'd remembered.

Fifteen minutes later, he walked through her door, holding two steaming cups. A friendly smile spread across his face, without any traces of the smolder from the night before or the tension from the morning. "I put some peppermint creamer in yours."

"Thanks." His catering to her preference was surprising. Not everyone made an effort to remember like he did. She pressed her hand over her growling stomach. "Did you have lunch yet?"

"No. I spent the morning on computer issue after computer issue. Hungry? Want to break out of this joint and grab something?"

"Uh... Sure." Maybe the near-kiss had been a fluke, brought on by close contact and her bruised ego wanting to see what wasn't there. She could buy that. And maybe he'd felt sorry for her, and had gotten caught up in the sharing of cocoa and pizza and linked arms and happy smiles. Yes, that must have been it.

"Is Mexican okay? Hot and spicy to counter the cold and snow."

"Sounds perfect."

They went to collect Damon and Aidan, then the

four of them headed out. She sat beside Hunter, both in Damon's car and at the restaurant. There weren't any awkward moments or heavy pauses, just him, as friendly as he'd always been. Obviously, he'd reached the same realization as she.

On Thursday morning, Kira arrived early at the meeting place for the morning run group. When Damon and then Aidan arrived, she exited her car and joined them by the trail. Cold wind stole her breath. She ducked her face into her scarf. At times like this, winter felt downright mean.

A few guys from the hockey team trickled in. But no sign of Hunter. She stamped her sneakers against the frozen ground and clapped her hands together to thwart the numbness creeping in despite her gloves.

Finally, Hunter's car arrived. He climbed out with stiff movements. The hat pulled low over his ears and brows and jacket collar pulled high over his neck and mouth, framed the agony in his gaze. Damon and Aidan exchanged glances with Kira. They knew as well as she that Hunter would out-stubborn them all. Still, Damon would try to fix it. He wasn't officially in charge of the group, but he tended to take over, especially when it came to watching out for Aidan and Hunter, and the guys let him.

Damon waved his hand, commanding attention. "Since the wind chill is fucking freezing, we're cutting the run down to the three-mile loop today. Any complaints? No? Good. Then let's go."

He took off at an easy pace. Aidan joined him, winking at Kira as he jogged by. She waited as the hockey guys passed, and then smiled at Hunter—her usual buddy on the runs. "Ready?"

"Sure." Face grim, he stared at the path ahead of them and moved slower than usual. All his concentration seemed to be on putting one foot in front of the other. Hopefully, winter would hurry up and leave soon. The frigid temperatures weren't kind to Hunter's body, especially during their morning runs, but he insisted on keeping the routine.

For a few minutes, they didn't speak. Over the years, she'd learned when he needed quiet. Thankfully, someone had salted the path, so they didn't have to run through snow or worry about too many patches of ice. Slips and falls were common during the winter, but that was the last thing Hunter needed.

As one mile turned into two, she caught him wincing in time with his footfalls. Stubborn, stubborn, stubborn man. She slowed her pace. He cast a glance in her direction and then slowed to match her steps.

By the start of mile three, he was swearing under his breath, and she couldn't take the strained quiet or his obvious pain for another moment. "Do you want to stop and rest, or maybe finish the mile by walking it? Or is pushing through with running better? That way, you get this over with faster."

His head snapped in her direction and his blue eyes

iced over. He always brushed aside concern, down-playing and minimizing attention. "If I'm slowing you down, feel free to go on ahead."

Behind the anger and indignation, she saw the hurt.

They'd fallen well behind the rest of the group, and at this rate, she expected a few of them to turn around soon to check on Hunter and her. Seeing his friends running circles around him wouldn't make him feel any better. "All I'm trying to do is make sure you're comfortable."

"I'm comfortable. Everything is peachy." His pace increased, but his grimaces and grunts showed the effort it cost him.

"Doesn't look so peachy from here." She slowed down again. "Come on, Hunter, talk to me. What would make you feel better?"

"Stop fussing over me. Just drop it." The words heaved out, slamming into her as heavy and angry as a punch. He stopped running and leaned forward, hands braced on his thighs, then he began rubbing them. Ignoring her. Cutting her off.

"Have it your way." Annoyance and hurt fueling her muscles, she took off, sprinting.

As she came to the end of the loop, Damon and Aidan were heading in her direction. A glimpse of the parking lot showed the other guys getting into their cars and driving off.

Gaze on the trail, Damon peered over her shoulder. "Where's Hunter?"

"I left him at the third mile marker. He's a little

snappy today." Damn it, her voice was *not* going to catch. She cleared her throat and kicked at some snow lining the path.

"He snapped at you?" Damon's brows rose and disappeared under his cap, and his eyes glinted like steel. She recognized the look all too well. He could go from zero to bulldog in the blink of an eye.

She held up her hands to stop him from growling. "Relax. I snapped back. It's fine."

Aidan patted her shoulder and then stepped around her. "Our boy's in a lot of pain today. We'd better check on him. Kira, you coming?"

"I guess." She broke into a run, with Damon on her side and Aidan bringing up the rear.

Moving toward them, less than half a mile away, Hunter's tall figure ran unevenly down the path. Alone. All alone. No one else had braved the trail that morning except their group. All of her anger squeezed out of her heart, and it filled with sympathy. She shouldn't have left him alone.

"Can't be angry at him when I see him like this," Damon muttered, and then increased his pace. He reached Hunter first, with Kira and Aidan right behind.

Damon joined him on his left side, nudging Hunter toward the middle of the path. "Too damn cold for a run."

Aidan took the spot on Hunter's other side. "Maybe we should consider switching to swimming at the gym on days like this."

"A hot tub would feel good right about now," Hunter

agreed. He met her gaze, and regret flashed in that stormy blue.

Offering him a careful smile, she moved next to Aidan. Four across, they finished the remainder of the mile together.

After a few minutes of stretching out their muscles, Kira bade them goodbye and headed for her car. While it warmed up, she stayed beside it, stretching a little more.

Hunter's shadow fell over her. "Hey."

She dropped into a forward fold, then slowly rolled up to standing. "Hey. I'm sorry about what happened on the path."

He leaned on her car door. "No, I am. I shouldn't have snapped."

"You were in pain."

"Not an excuse. Can I bring you coffee and breakfast to make up for it?" Since Tuesday, Hunter had been stopping by her office with two coffees first thing in the morning. After he'd done his daily check-in on the Romeo situation, they'd sit at her desk discussing whatever had happened the previous evening—his hockey games, her yoga class, shows they'd watched—or whatever they hadn't covered during their morning run.

"You bring the coffees. I'll bring the breakfast." She extended the peace offering with a smile. Their morning coffee conversation was the best part of her day, and she wanted their normal back.

His features relaxed into a relieved smile. "Deal."

An hour later, after a hot shower and short commute,

Kira slipped into her office and bumped up the room temperature by ten degrees. She wanted the room nice and toasty before Hunter arrived.

She positioned his chair directly below the air duct and set out the foil-wrapped breakfast sandwich she'd picked up during the drive. Hopefully, the warmth of both would help him feel better.

The scent of coffee preceded him. He strode into the room, his gait still a little slower and stiffer than usual. Smile tight, he set the coffees on the desk and then gripped both chair arms as he lowered himself onto the seat. "Thanks for breakfast."

Kira resisted the urge to curl her hand into his. But she *had* to say something. "I have a bottle of pain reliever and a heating pad in my desk if you need them."

Dark resentment flashed across his face before that tough warrior mask slipped into place. He sipped his coffee and pointed to her computer screen. "I'm fine. Any word from Romeo?"

She stifled a sigh and switched to the topic he wanted to discuss. "Just a message wishing me good morning, and he added in a poem, which just so happens to be my favorite, Lord Byron's *She Walks In Beauty*."

"So, Byron from Byron, hmm? Clever. You don't think this Romeo guy's name really is Byron, do you?" He tapped a blunt finger against her screen.

She swallowed more coffee. "It could be. Other men do have that name, you know."

"What's this poem about, anyway?" He leaned over her shoulder, gaze intent as he scanned the words on the screen. "You've never mentioned him sending you poetry before."

"He usually sends me a poem once a week, saying that he read it and was reminded of me."

Hunter made a low sound deep in his chest. "Is that what you want? Some guy who sends you another man's words instead of his own?"

Irritation flared at his question. Taking a deep breath, she set her mug on the desk. "What I want is someone who will be there for me no matter what, who cares enough to pay attention to my likes and dislikes, and who makes me laugh and start my day with a smile."

He glanced at the words again. "I can see why someone would think of you when reading these lines. When you smile, the whole room lights up."

Pleasure swelled, then increased at the sincerity in his gaze. "Hunter…"

His phone buzzed. He glanced at the screen and sighed. "I have to go."

"But you just got here."

"Duty calls." His face twisted into a grimace, and his knuckles turned white as he pushed himself out of the chair. Pocketing his phone, he lifted his coffee. "I'll see you tonight. Dinner's at six-thirty, right?"

"Yep."

Kira watched his slow movements. He and Aidan were always included in every Kallis family dinner and every holiday. Aidan didn't have family close by, and Hunter's relationship with most of his family was strained. He almost never spoke about it, but she knew enough, and that he blamed himself, and her heart broke for him every time she thought about it. So, she was especially grateful that her parents had basically adopted Aidan and him as part of the family. Tonight's dinner to celebrate her parents' thirty-eighth wedding anniversary wasn't any exception. Her parents had issued the invite, delivered at a family dinner, weeks earlier.

"Hunter…"

The scowl on his face deepened and his free hand pressed into the side of his thigh. "What?"

She held back the suggestion for him to take a personal day and rest his legs. He'd never listen, and she didn't want to fight with him again. But if she found her way to the IT department a few times under the guise of coffee runs, and needing to stretch her legs, then she could keep an eye on him. "Thank you for the coffee. And don't forget to take the breakfast sandwich with you."

A smile formed despite the tension tightening his face, and something close to relief passed through his gaze. "You're welcome. And, thanks."

Twelve hours later, Kira stood at the island in her parents' kitchen, helping her mom dish out dessert while Damon and her dad loaded the dinner plates into the dishwasher. Anniversary cards covered the space in front of her. She picked up the one she'd given her parents. Two interlocking hearts graced the front of the card. The card shop had been a depressing reminder that romance was everywhere—except in her life.

Her mom handed her a plate. "So, how's the dating?"

She sliced into the chocolate cake, concentrating on cutting even pieces. "Well, everything I've read says to make your life interesting first. I have that—a job I love, a great group of friends, fun hobbies. I don't understand why finding someone is so hard."

"Maybe you're thinking about it too much. I believe you'll meet the right person once you stop looking."

"So, I'm supposed to sit at home and wait? The only guy I'll meet that way is the mailman."

"Our mailman isn't married. He's very nice and probably about your age. If you'd like, I can show him your picture the next time I see him. I'm sure Nana would do it for you, too. With the size of our family, we could cover nearly every mail and package delivery route in the tri-state area."

In spite of herself, Kira couldn't hold back the laugh. "I can picture it. All the little old ladies in our family turning into matchmakers, waylaying the workers and waving fliers with my information."

"Don't worry, Princess. I won't let them." Her dad turned from the sink and swept her mom into a waltz around the room. He'd done that so many times over the years. The way they looked at each other, still so much in love, was beautiful.

Watching their parents, Damon joined Kira and

picked up two plates laden with thick slices of cake. "I'm still not happy about you doing this whole online thing."

She licked icing from the tip of her thumb. "You've essentially employed a babysitter for me, so I'd think you'd be able to relax."

He frowned. "Hunter's not a sitter. He's more like… a guard."

After Hunter's seeming frustration over Byron that morning, she didn't want to bother him anymore. "I don't need a guard, and I'm sure he has better things to do."

"Actually, I don't." Hunter came up behind them, holding two glasses of wine. Aidan and his dog, Chance, followed behind. Hunter extended one of the glasses to her. "You left this in the dining room."

Her fingers brushed his when she accepted her glass. She couldn't ignore the tingle of awareness, or pretend it was due to static electricity. Holding her gaze, he smiled, a sexy a half-smile that weakened her knees, and the smoldering intensity in his gaze sent a tug straight through to her core. The same smoldering intensity he'd had when she'd dropped off lunch to him at noon and again when she'd delivered coffee at three. The same smoldering intensity he'd had the night of their near-kiss. Her heartbeat stuttered, and her mouth went dry.

Damon set the plates down with a clatter and then tapped Hunter on the shoulder. "Let's go. You and me."

She blinked at his sharp tone. "Where are you going?"

"Outside." He waited for Hunter to exit and then pulled the door closed behind them.

Her parents stopped dancing, and her mom glanced over her shoulder. "What's going on with them?"

Shaking her head, Kira set aside her knife. She took two steps in the direction of the door. "I don't know, but I'd better find out."

Aidan's touch on her arm halted her movement. Concerning creasing his gaze, he glanced out the backyard window. When he turned back to Kira, the lines on his face faded. Whatever he'd seen in the yard had eased his worry. "I'd wait a few minutes. Let them talk."

"But—"

"Trust me. They need to clear the air."

"About what?"

He reached for a slice of cake. "You."

CHAPTER FOUR

Chilly night air slapped his skin. Hunter tightened his muscles against the cold. He followed Damon halfway across the yard. Fresh snow crunched under his shoes. Under the floodlights, his shadow stretched tall across the covered lawn. "What's up?"

Damon rounded on him. "What the hell's going on with you and my sister?"

Hunter raised his hands but held his ground. "I'm checking into the guy who's been emailing her. Like I told you."

"That's not all. I saw the way you were looking at her in there."

"Nothing happened." Nothing, thanks to that ill-timed phone call on Sunday. He sighed. "I'm not going to lie to you. I like her. She's amazing."

"She's... Damn it, she's my sister. And you're my best friend." He pinched the bridge of his nose. "And I don't need any more to worry about."

Message received, loud and clear. Clenching his jaw, Hunter turned toward the house. Light streamed from the windows. His home away from home. Damon's parents treated him like a son. Damon was like his brother. He couldn't jeopardize his relationship with them. And he'd never risk hurting Kira, or them. He had to stop his feelings, somehow. "You don't have to worry. Nothing's going to happen. I won't dump my baggage on her or you or your family and make a mess. She deserves better than me."

"That's not what I meant. You're one of the good guys. I trust you. If she has to be with someone, I want it to be with someone I trust."

He inhaled slow and deep. Damon's words soothed something inside him, but not enough for him to pursue Kira. "I appreciate your blessing, but she's still your sister and I wouldn't do anything to hurt her or you. I'll make sure she's okay with this online guy, but that's it."

"What's going on with him?"

"Don't know. But from what I've seen so far, if he's real, then he's an idiot. And if he's a fake, well, then I'll want to hunt him down and kick his ass."

"We both will." Damon shoved his hands into his pockets and kicked at a loose stone on the patio. "Nobody hurts her and gets away with it."

"Agreed." And that was why he needed to ditch these feelings. But they surfaced every time he saw her or thought about her.

Gaze curious, Damon cocked his head and studied at

him. "If you like her, you should speak up. Don't let this online thing get in your way."

"I told you, man. It can't happen. You know what I go through. No one I'm interested in needs that."

"Come on. Cut yourself a break. I think you—"

"No." He barked out the word. Heat flushed through his system. "Not happening. Enough talking about this. Kira's out of my league and off my radar. Done. We don't need to say anything else about it. It's a non-issue."

The back door opened, and Kira stepped outside. Her concerned glance was at odds with her casual tone. "Dad's threatening to eat your slices of cake."

"We're coming," Damon called out. He leaned toward Hunter and murmured, "Non-issue? Off your radar? If that's the way you want it, then I won't keep harping on it."

He cuffed Hunter on the back and headed for the house.

Rather than following her brother inside, Kira strode toward Hunter. She rubbed her hands over her arms and kept her dark chocolate gaze locked on him. "What's going on with Damon?"

He rubbed his hand over the back of his neck. "He just wanted an update on the online thing. That's all."

"I hope that's all. He seemed pretty wound up." Doubt clouded her features, but she didn't press him any further. Her arms and legs shivered, and her teeth chattered. That thin sweater wasn't enough.

His hands itched to rub warmth into her skin. "We should go inside. You're freezing."

She took one of his hands between both of hers and gently squeezed. "Are you sure he didn't say anything he shouldn't have? You know him, sometimes he gets overprotective and overreacts. I don't want him barking at you over the Clicked Hearts stuff."

He soaked up the heat in her gentle caress. "You're sweet to worry about me, but Damon and I are fine. I promise."

"You're a good friend to him. And to me. Thank you."

Good friends didn't feel the way he felt about Kira. Good friends didn't want *more*. Good friends knew where to draw boundary lines. He needed to set his with electrified fences. "You can always count on me to be here for you."

"I do. I've known that for years. Do you know how lucky that makes me feel?" She grabbed hold of his other hand and gave it the same treatment.

He felt the contact all the way down to his toes. Pulling away left him cold, in more ways than one. "We should go inside before your lips start turning blue."

She led the way to the house, and he took a deep breath to settle down. Enemy bullets hadn't killed him, but those soft touches would.

Two hours past the close of business, Hunter strolled through the nearly empty Kallis Factory building, his thoughts on an evening of watching some hockey. Friday night and the weekend stretched out before him. Hunter and Aidan were hunkered down at Aidan's place, in the early planning stage of a huge HR project. Maybe he'd pick up a six-pack and stop by. He could watch the game there, and they'd need a break eventually. It was a good way to usher in the celebration of the end of the work week.

Light shone from Kira's office. He changed directions, heading toward her open door. Stuck putting out fires all day, he hadn't seen her since their morning coffee.

"Kira? What are you still doing here?"

At his words, she spun away from the window. A pencil stuck out of her messy bun. Her deep purple sweater and dark jeans hinted at her curves. The hint left a lot to the imagination, and his imagination had no trouble filling in the rest. With a frown, she set her phone on the desk. "I have two tickets to a wine and canvas class tonight. I'd completely forgotten about it until I received the reminder email this afternoon. The tickets are non-refundable, and I can't find anyone to go with me."

"What about Romeo?"

"He hasn't been online, and there isn't any time now. The class starts in half an hour. Everyone I've called is busy. It's really not the kind of thing I want to go to alone."

He'd never tried one of those fancy painting events, and maybe more close-proximity with Kira wasn't smart, but he was in a position to help her. Hadn't he promised that he'd always be there for her? "I'll go."

Her eyes widened and then sparkled as her expression shifted from disappointed to excited. "Really?"

"Sure."

Her smile lit up the room. "Thanks. I'll spring for dinner afterward. There's a sushi restaurant close to the studio."

"Sounds good." Not that he'd let her pay for the meal. The tickets for the class were enough.

He followed her to the studio—a tiny brick storefront in a newly revitalized part of Buffalo. When they walked inside, three identical rows of canvases and supplies lined the middle of the room. The majority of the people signed up to the class appeared to be couples. And the painting they were supposed to recreate was a giant gleaming heart on a colorful background.

Kira motioned him closer. Twin spots of color appeared on her cheeks. "To be honest, when I'd purchased these, I really thought I'd have someone in my life. So I picked the romantic heart painting. But if you want to paint something else, I'm sure you can. We get to keep our canvases."

He made a game face. "I'll give it a go. Why don't we grab some wine and find a seat?"

Glasses in hand, they settled into two seats in the middle of the center row. To his left sat a couple on their first date, and to Kira's right were a couple who'd recently celebrated their tenth wedding anniversary.

The instructor gave them a crash course, step-by-step process for how to paint the image on the canvas of the painting and promised they'd have a decent piece if they followed her directions. She then ended her speech by telling everyone to "above all else, relax, have fun, and follow your heart," and pointed to the painting they were supposed to copy.

The first step was painting the background color. Kira selected pink and red, and Hunter went for green and brown. Sliding the brush back and forth along the canvas was soothing. Bold arches in tan made up the halves of his heart. He glanced at Kira's heart, formed by graceful strokes of purple.

All around them, couples were flirting, touching, and being romantic. Torture, when he couldn't do the same. He asked Kira about one of the marketing campaigns she'd recently began. Keeping the conversation on work made their evening seem less like a date.

When they ran out of work topics, he turned to the one thing guaranteed to remind him that she wasn't supposed to be anything more than a friend. "You said Romeo wasn't online this afternoon but was there any word from him since I saw you this morning?"

"Yep, we're going to video chat tomorrow afternoon." She smiled and swirled more paint onto the canvas.

Jealousy streaked through him, as vibrant as the red coloring her painting. "What time?"

"Four o'clock."

He concentrated on blending the thick brush strokes. The image looked like pea soup melting into mud. "Okay. I'll come by your place fifteen minutes early."

"You don't have to, it's just a chat."

"I want to see this guy. What if he's not who he says he is?"

Her hand reached over and stopped his movement. He twisted toward her and met her serious brown gaze. "Please take this in a nice way, but I won't be able to relax if you're there."

"Why?"

She raised a brow. "Would you really want me hanging around when you're trying to talk to a woman?"

No other woman could hold a candle to her. "Damon asked me to look out for you. Let me come and see the guy, then I'll get out of your way, I swear."

Her mouth opened, then closed, and then she sighed a soft, slow exhale. "Fine. But he can't be like this with every guy I date. He wasn't like this before."

"I think it's just because of what happened with Ursula." He dabbed more color onto the heart, then held the brush to his finished canvas. "What do you think?"

Kira's heart, a mosaic of reds, pinks, and purples, looked way nicer that his camouflage one of olive green, brown, and tan. But neither of their paintings looked anywhere near as good as their instructor's masterpiece.

She wrinkled her nose at her artwork. "I think we might need to do this a few more times."

If she was willing, then so was he.

As friends.

Only, telling himself that he was just hanging out with a friend wasn't working too well. He needed to keep himself in check, or he'd end up doing something stupid, like almost kissing her again.

CHAPTER FIVE

Excitement about the video chat carried Kira through Saturday morning and into the afternoon. She dressed in slim-fitting pants the color of cranberries and a sheer, long-sleeved black and white polka dot blouse over a white tank top. Chunky gold bracelets and a thick braided necklace added some shine. And even though Byron wouldn't see them, she'd slipped on camel colored suede heels that gave her an extra five inches in height. She left her hair loose and spent way too much time on her makeup, highlighting, contouring, and adding gold and bronze shimmer to her eyes. The last touch was a slick pink lip gloss the color of crushed raspberries.

Nerves fluttered her stomach, and her heart pounded a steady beat. She poured a healthy splash of white wine into a crystal goblet and took a fortifying sip.

Her doorbell rang at three-forty-five. Hunter. Right on time. She opened the door with the wine in her hand.

A brown leather jacket several shades darker than his hair covered a light gray sweater. Her gaze roamed lower, over jeans faded perfectly at the knees, and the brown shoes she'd helped him pick out the year before. "Come in."

His gaze swept from her head to her feet. "Whoa."

She stepped back, glancing down at her shirt. "What? Is something wrong?"

"No." He shut the door at his back and then shoved his hands into his pockets.

Biting her lip, she tugged on a strand of hair. Maybe she should have curled it… "Do I look okay?"

He performed a second, slower study. His eyes darkened and then latched onto hers. "Better than any model I've ever seen."

She smiled, buoyed by the compliment. "Thanks."

He didn't look too happy about it. "Nervous?"

"A little. I'm not sure what to expect." She sipped more wine, then gestured to her glass. "Want some?"

He shook his head. "Let's give Romeo a call."

"I thought we'd sit at the kitchen table." She led the way into the kitchen, grabbed a bottle of water from the fridge, and lobbed it to him in an easy underhand toss.

Hunter laid his jacket over the back of his chair and sat by her side but out of camera range. His movements were abrupt, almost impatient.

She waited until his gaze connected with hers. "If you have someplace else to be or something else to do, don't worry about staying here just to appease Damon."

"I'm fine." He twisted off the cap and downed half the contents of his water bottle.

"All right..." Signing into the video chat took less than thirty seconds. She focused her attention on the screen and gripped her hands tight together in her lap.

Minutes ticked by. No sign of Byron. She couldn't bring herself to meet Hunter's gaze. If Byron was a no-show again... She logged into the dating site and sent out a message.

Brown-Eyed-Girl: Hey, did you forget? We're supposed to be video chatting right now.

A minute later, his response appeared.

Real-Life-Romeo: Having audio and camera problems on my end. Bummer, right?

"Bummer? *Bummer*?" She turned toward Hunter. "In your expert opinion, why isn't that part of his computer working?"

"My expert opinion isn't feeling very kindhearted right now. It's probably in the best interest of our friendship if I don't answer that question." His hand crushed the now-empty water bottle. "Tell him to call you. He can video chat through the dating site's app or a ton of other apps on his phone. If he can manage to operate his phone correctly."

Embarrassment warred with annoyance. Sarcasm wasn't something she'd often experienced from Hunter. She turned back to the computer.

Brown-Eyed-Girl: Then let's try the video chat on the phone. Try through Clicked Hearts app first?

"Okay, we'll see." Twirling the stem of her glass kept her hands busy while she waited for his response.

Real-Life-Romeo: Trying now...

Kira wiped damn palms on her thighs and opened the app on her phone. And waited.

Hunter pointed to her computer screen. "He sent a message."

Real-Life-Romeo: The chat app isn't working. Sorry, love.

"It's working just fine on both your phone and computer." Hunter rolled his shoulders, looking like he wanted to crush the computer the same way he'd destroyed the water bottle.

Brown-Eyed-Girl: We could try another app. Or just give me a regular call. We can at least hear each other's voices.

His response appeared in less than a minute.

Real-Life-Romeo: Just tried calling. That's not working either. Sorry, love.

A growl sounded in Hunter's throat. "Where the hell is he, a cave? Tell him you'll call him if he's having problems."

She typed the message and then dialed the number he'd given her before their ice skating misadventure. It rang five times, then went to voicemail. The outgoing message wasn't his voice, just an automated voice stating the number dialed and instructions to leave a message. Holding in a sigh, Kira sent a text again.

Brown-Eyed-Girl: Still there? I called and got voice-mail. I'm calling again now.

No response. She dialed again. Again, the call went to voicemail. Giving him the benefit of the doubt was starting to wear thin. Kira set the phone aside. "Maybe he's trying to find a better spot to call. I'll give him a few minutes."

Five minutes passed. She drained her wine.

Fingers drumming on the edge of the table, Hunter grabbed her phone and then dialed. Thirty seconds later, he pulled the phone away from his ear, scowling at the device. "Voice mail again."

"What the hell?" She sent a message asking Byron to confirm the number he'd supplied.

Five more minutes of awkward silence later, his reply appeared.

Real-Life-Romeo: Sorry about that. Listen, talking today isn't going to work. I have to go into the office. My boss just called. He's a real hard ass.

"Unbelievable," Hunter muttered under his breath. "The call from the boss goes through, but yours doesn't?"

"Maybe his boss left him a voicemail."

"Yeah, but you still have to call your voicemail to get the messages."

"True." Any lingering excitement she'd felt flatlined.

"Where does he work?"

"He told me he works for a tech company. He does something with computers."

Hunter's eyes widened and his expression jumped from shock to disbelief to derision. "Wait. He does something with computers? Even if his computer wasn't working, most tech guys have more than one computer at home. You've seen my place, you know all of the stuff I have laying around. He's either the most inept IT guy ever or he's lying his ass off."

Her patience snapped. "Maybe he's not in the IT department. I don't know."

Brown-Eyed-Girl: What is it that do you do again?

Real-Life-Romeo: Sorry, love. That's classified. :wink:

"Seriously?" Brow raised, incredulous, Hunter met her gaze, shaking his head. "You need to get rid of this guy."

"He could be telling the truth. Or maybe he's married. Or maybe he's just some kid goofing off." Altogether, things didn't add up well. Embarrassment and hurt scraped over her heart. The possibility of being played by this unknown man made her feel equal parts naive and stupid. Her chair scraped against the floor as she rose. Working hard to keep her emotions under control, she walked into the living room and then paused in the front entryway. "Thanks for coming over."

"We're done here?" Still seated, Hunter shook his head. "No way. You need to call him out on things."

"Hunter, I'm really not in the mood to do this anymore. Thank you for trying to help me. I'll see you at work on Monday."

"You're done with him?" His voice ticked up and the dark storm clouding his features lightened.

She shrugged. It was either that or hit something. "For tonight, I'm done with everything."

He turned to her computer and his fingers pecked at the keys.

"What are you doing?" She crossed to him but Hunter tugged the laptop closer to himself.

"I'm telling him you're going out to dinner tonight."

"And what's that supposed to do?"

"I want to see if that changes his reaction."

"Fine." She leaned over his shoulder and read the conversation on the screen.

Brown-Eyed-Girl: Too bad about having to work. I'm grabbing dinner with a friend.

Real-Life-Romeo: Have fun.

Brown-Eyed-Girl: Oh, I will. :wink: He'll be here any minute. Gotta get ready.

Real-Life-Romeo: Him???

"You made it sound like I have a date." She reached for the computer, but Hunter stood and held it over his head.

"So what? If he's interested, that'll push him to action."

She tugged at his bicep. "Give me the computer."

He stared at her for a moment and then lowered the laptop to the table, but shifted his body to block her from grabbing hold of the device. "Don't respond to him. Let it go for today and wait until tomorrow."

"I don't like lying." She hated deception of any sort —both in business and in her personal life—and made it a point to always strive for honesty.

His scowl had lightened, but tension still lined his face. "It wasn't lying. I'm taking you to dinner."

"You don't have to do that. I don't need pity because my stupid video date didn't work out and the guy might be a flighty, lying jerk." She needed time alone to process everything that had happened.

He crossed his arms over his chest. "You're cute when you pout."

She pressed her lips together, banking the fire of frustration. "I'm not pouting."

"Not anymore. Come on, don't make me eat alone. Aidan and Damon are working on that huge HR project again tonight. If left to my own devices, I'll end up nuking a frozen burrito and probably bugging the hell out of them." His raised brows and his persuasive words broke through her resolve.

No matter what, he could always lighten her mood. "All right. But it'll be my treat, as a thank you."

"We'll debate that part later."

"I'm not backing down." With a smile, she reached around him. Lightning fast, his hand closed over her wrist, trapping her in his heat.

Scant inches separated them and he bent toward her, eliminating all but a few inches. "Promise me. No responding to him. No trying to correct what I implied."

Awareness snapped along her skin, radiating from the point of contact. She took a moment to steady herself. "I'm only shutting down the computer."

"Good." After a long moment, he released his hold

and stepped aside. "Now let's get some food. I'm starving."

"Where did you want to go?"

"How about the Greek place you really like?"

Her smile bloomed. "Really? Give me a few seconds to get ready."

He nodded.

She hurried to her bedroom, spritzed on perfume and swapped her heels for black suede boots that hit just above her knee. And realized she was more excited about dinner with Hunter than she'd been about the video chat with Byron.

She sat down hard on the edge of her bed.

Hunter.

Maybe the reason no other guy had completely captured her interest was because her interest was solely in the dark blond standing in her kitchen. Had been for years, if she were really honest with herself. Caring and attraction ran deep. Outside of that almost kiss, he'd never acted interested in her. But no—there had been times when she'd seen something smoldering in his gaze. Several times, in fact, over the last few weeks.

Maybe he wasn't into her.

But what if he was?

CHAPTER SIX

The restaurant was packed, but the owner, Athena, was a good friend of Kira's mom. She greeted Kira with a warm hug and sized up Hunter like Kira expected her own family would do with a potential boyfriend. In less than five minutes, they were seated at a small table in a quieter corner, close enough that if they reached across the table, they could touch each other's faces.

Hunter smiled at her like she was the only woman in the room. She suddenly felt shy. This was way more like a date than any of the countless meals they'd shared over the years. Their knees brushed under the table, but neither shifted away. Their hands inched closer together drawn by an almost magnetic force. Fingers brushed as they scooped up tangy hummus with warm, fresh pita bread. He offered her a taste of his Chicken Souvlakia, raising a forkful to her lips. She did the same with her swordfish steak.

Unlike her Clicked Hearts match-ups, being with

Hunter felt right and effortless. When their dinner plates were cleared away, Athena delivered a large piece of baklava with two forks, and two heart-shaped cups of cappuccino. She winked as she served them and Kira had a feeling her mom would hear about the meal long before she and Hunter said goodnight.

Hunter's gaze flicked to the cozy shared dessert. "I guess they're ready for Valentine's Day."

"I'm sure." She wasn't. Eight days to go until her self-imposed deadline. She raised the cup to her lips and took a sip.

He leaned toward her. "You have a little foam... right... here." He brushed his thumb just below her lip.

A shiver, more frothy than the foam he'd wiped away, danced down her spine. "Thanks."

He lowered his hand to rest on the table, inches from hers, and she wondered if she dared bridge the tiny gap.

Her phone's message alert sounded, startling her. Probably her mom. News traveled fast. She ignored it and picked up her fork to taste the honeyed sweetness of the rich pastry.

The alert sounded again.

Then again.

Kira set her fork aside. "Do you mind if I check my messages? I hate doing that when I'm with someone, but it never goes off like this and I'm worried something's wrong."

"Go ahead."

She glanced at the screen. All of the messages had come from Byron. A funny feeling unsettled her stomach. Definitely not pleasure. More like awkward annoyance. Without a word, she returned the phone to her purse. "So, where were we?"

Hunter's blue eyes were trained on her face. "What's wrong? You don't look happy."

"I'm fine."

He lowered his brows. "I know you too well to believe that. You're pressing your lips together, and you have that little crease in your forehead that you get when you're stressed."

"It's nothing important." She smiled and nudged the plate toward him. "Isn't this good? I've tried making it, but mine never comes out quite this perfect."

He crossed his arms over his chest and had a stubborn tilt to his chin. "That stress mark is still there, so I think it's important."

With a sigh, she rolled her shoulders. "Fine. Byron sent three messages."

"Three?"

"Apologizing like crazy for messing up today. He wants to try it again tomorrow, says he's free to talk anytime."

A smirk flashed across his features. "I figured he'd do something like that. If he's free to talk, then he should be free to meet up."

"I guess, but I was planning on coming to your game. Damon gets so riled up playing the Dragons. And after meeting that Waverly guy last weekend, I want to be there to see you guys beat them."

"I can't wait to get on the ice." An unholy glee

shined in his eyes. "I got hip-checked into their bench the last time we played them. I ended up catching a punch to the jaw and a hard slam to the side of my helmet."

Picturing the punches turned her stomach. She reached across the table and laid her hand over his upturned palm. "I'm sorry."

A half-smile curled his lips. "Thanks, but it wasn't your fault."

"Still… It was Waverly, wasn't it?"

"He threw a jab-cross combination. The ref didn't see it."

She squeezed his fingers. "I knew something was up from the look you had on your face when we saw him. We should take his suggestion and put me in the game. But instead of distracting them with fancy skating moves, I want to knock him out."

"Thanks for sticking up for me. You'd make a cute enforcer." His thumb brushed over hers, back and forth, in a slow slide. His gaze drifted from their joined hands to her face. She watched his sensuous mouth while he spoke, and wondered if his tongue would flick across her skin in the same rhythm… For a moment, she lost track of the conversation. All concentration settled on that small strip of skin. "But I wouldn't want you on the ice with him. I don't want you anywhere near him. If anyone hurts you, they'll answer to me. That includes Byron."

"I don't think you have to worry about him hurting me."

He laced their fingers together. "But I do worry about that. I want to see this guy. Ask him to meet you at the game tomorrow."

"I don't think so."

"Why not?"

"Because I'm not all that into him anymore." As close as they'd grown over the years, as comfortable as she felt with him, she couldn't tell him how she felt. Instead, she focused her gaze on his and gave his hand a gentle squeeze.

His eyes darkened. He opened his mouth, but before he could speak, the waitress delivered their check. He released his hold on her hand and dug for his wallet.

Kira shook her head and reached for the folder. "I said dinner was on me, remember?"

"I invited you, so it's my treat." He quickly fanned out a few bills and shoved them in the folder and then flagged down the waitress.

"Hunter…"

"Ready to go?" He shrugged into his jacket.

Feeling silly, and more than a little disappointed, she slipped into her coat. Maybe she had imagined the need in his gaze.

They didn't talk much during the short drive back to her place. Hunter had cranked the heater full-blast and ratcheted up the radio as if intentionally shutting down communication. When they pulled into her driveway, she unbuckled her seatbelt and turned to him, and silenced the radio. "Thanks for dinner and… for tonight." She paused, getting up her nerve. "Do you want to come in?"

She'd expected him to turn her down, but he agreed. "Sure. There's something I want to say, anyway."

Anticipation quickened her steps to the house. Debating between offering him wine or coffee, and whether it really mattered, Kira unlocked the door, and then waited for him to enter before closing and locking it behind him.

As soon as they stepped into her living room, he stopped her. "I really am sorry about what happened today with Byron."

"I'm not letting it bother me." She tossed her coat on a chair and set her purse beside it, then set about turning on lights, brightening the space with their soft glow.

He caught hold of her hand. Strong fingers drew her in, closer to his warmth and the wide expanse of his chest. "If I were him, I'd sure as hell never leave you hanging. Nothing could keep me away."

Her breath caught in her chest. He lowered his head toward hers. She'd read the intention in his eyes, and was ready to meet it head-on. "Nothing?"

"Nothing."

His hand cupped her jaw. He paused a breath away, and then his lips ghosted against hers—feather light touches, over and over, rubbing, teasing, and driving her crazy.

She needed more. Kira dove her hands into his hair and tugged on the short blond strands until Hunter's mouth finally fused with her, hot and hard. He groaned as his hands curled into her shoulder and hip, holding her to him, keeping her close.

This. This. This. The word chanted over and over in her mind. This was what she'd been searching for. Sparks. Fireworks. A symphony of sensations.

Rising onto her toes, she pressed herself against him. Every part of him lined up with her, and eagerness to explore every inch of him pounded through her in time with her heartbeats. She slid one hand down his neck and to his chest, roaming over tight pecs. The soft wool of his sweater couldn't conceal the hard muscles beneath her hand.

His tongue stroked against hers, and her hips rocked in time with his thrusts. She couldn't get close enough to him.

He lifted his head. Breathing hard, his gaze raked over her face.

She stared back at the face she'd grown to care so much for over the years. He looked as dazed and surprised as she felt. Who knew this punch of passion, this torrent of feelings, had been hiding between them all this time?

Hunter traced a fingertip down her cheek. "Kiss me again."

CHAPTER SEVEN

Hunter held Kira in his arms, and damn it, she felt good there. He grazed his lips along her jaw, along her throat, to the slope of her shoulder. Her murmurs and hands fisted in his hair drove him hotter and his need higher.

Breathing her in, he reversed the trail and worked his way back to her mouth. Soft lips curved, then opened under his. A satisfied groan rumbled low in his throat. Kissing her was quickly becoming his favorite activity. He was made for it, and from the stirrings in his body, a hell of a lot more with her.

Her scent surrounded him, her soft skin and her curves called to him, and the rest of the world faded away. It hadn't been this way with anyone else. An all-consuming fire, a need in his blood, a sudden click of broken pieces snapping into place.

He spun her in a slow circle, then his gaze landed on the framed family photos decorating the mantel over the fire place. There were several of Damon and Kira with their parents, Stan and Nadia. He and Aidan even graced a few. His favorite was a picture that included Aidan and him with Kira's family—taken last Thanksgiving at her parents' home.

They'd given him everything. He owed them huge. He couldn't risk losing them, or Damon, or the family he'd finally found. He would lose them, he'd lose everything if he ended up hurting her.

And he would end up hurting her—that much was a given.

The thought iced over the heat of passion. He gentled his hands and smoothed the back of her shirt. Kira gazed up at him, her chocolate-brown eyes misted with need. He took a step back and rubbed his hand through his hair. "I wish I'd met you first. Before I met Damon."

"Why?"

"Because then you wouldn't be my best friend's sister." He sighed. Jumbled emotions tangled with his thoughts. How could he make her understand that she was too important to risk? "You'd just be this awesome woman I met."

She wrinkled her brow. "I really don't understand what you're saying."

"As much as I want you, we can't do this."

Her fingers curled into her palms. The sparkle faded from her eyes. "Can't do what? Kiss? Touch? Be together?"

"Damon's always going to be a part of my life. Hell —he saved my life. If it weren't for him, I wouldn't be here. If you and I started something and things don't work out between us—if I ended up hurting you—I can't do that to you or to him or to your family."

"So regardless of the chemistry between us," she gestured to their rumpled clothes and hair, "you're saying nothing can happen?"

He shook his head. He couldn't let himself dwell on how right she'd felt in his arms. "I care too much about you."

"You care too much?" Her laugh was hollow. "What a lame let down."

"It's not. I can never repay Damon for what he's done for me. He's taken care of Aidan and me since we got out. He was my lifeline for years. Your family accepted me, gave me a job, gave me a purpose when my family had given up on me. They became my family. I've worked hard for years to show them how much I appreciate it all. I depend on them, need them. I can't risk losing any of that."

"You wouldn't lose that." Her eyes softened. She reached for him, then pulled back her hand when he didn't move. It fell limp to her side.

"If I end up hurting you, I would. I'd lose everything."

"Why are you so convinced you'd hurt me? We've been friends for years without many issues."

"Being friends is one thing, being in a romantic relationship is another, and being in one twenty-four-seven is a whole other level. I'm damaged goods. I'm not the easiest person to be with, and sure as hell not the easiest person to live with. Some days I'm beyond moody when the PTSD kicks in. Some days, the nerve pain gets so bad that I snap—it happens often. You've seen it over the years. Hell, you've been on the receiving end of it, and that guts me. The last thing I want to do is snarl at you, change you, or hurt you. But it's inevitable. Eventually, you'd regret you're with me. You deserve someone who's whole. That's not me."

"Hunter... Like I said, we've been friends for years. The few times you've snapped at me, I could see you were in pain, and I knew the pain was causing it. And yes, I have noticed your dark moods. And on top of that, it's incredibly frustrating when you won't let anyone help you, so I'm sure we'd fight, because I want to help you and if we were together then I wouldn't back down, but—"

"You know that saying, 'you hurt the ones you love the most'?" He waited until she nodded. Everything she said filled him with hope and fear. Fear won out, because damn it, he knew better. Life with him wasn't easy, and someone as special as Kira deserved only the best. "I know that's true. I've seen the hurt in your eyes when I've snapped or snarled. A relationship can't happen between us."

"There's no changing your mind, then?" Her voice, husky with emotion, made him want to forget good reason.

"No."

For long moments they stared at each other. The

only sounds came from the wind whistling through the trees and the click of the heater.

Hunter didn't know what else to say, but he wasn't ready to go either. He shoved his hands into his pockets and inwardly cursed at the unfairness of the situation. The tingling pain in his thighs returned, a painful reminder of part of his daily struggles.

Kira crossed her arms over her chest. Her foot tapped the hardwood floor. Her gaze swirled with emotions—hurt, anger, and something he couldn't name. "You know, friends can have falling outs and hurt each other just as much as someone in a romantic relationship."

Something about her tone raised a warning flag. "What are you saying?"

"Since you're so worried about hurting me, the only way to guarantee that doesn't happen is for us to stop being friends." Her voice hardened. "I'll go back to only being Damon's sister."

He moved a step closer. "What are you saying?"

She backed up, putting more distance between them. "You and I can't be running buddies anymore. Or have coffee dates at my desk. Or lunches or dinners together. Or wine and canvas classes. Or texts. Or phone calls. Or any contact that's not work-related. From here on out, we'll be business acquaintances only. We'll see each other whenever it's necessary, but that's it."

At her words, cold stole over his bones. "I don't want to lose you."

Hurt and anger in her eyes, she strode to her front

door and flung it open. "You can't have it both ways. Maybe you can ignore the way you feel about me, but I sure as hell can't about you. Knowing that, it's going to be too hard to be around you and try to pretend I don't feel it. And since you're so adamant in your decision, I don't want to waste years continuing to do all of that friendship stuff with you, wishing and wondering if maybe someday you'll change your mind. I deserve better than that."

Rooted to his spot, he stared at her. "What the hell just happened here?"

"Look at it like a system reboot." Her hand trembled against the knob. "Please go."

Hunter grabbed his jacket off the chair and headed for the door, head swimming, thoughts speeding. Once in the threshold, he turned, but Kira was already nudging the door closed. She clicked the lock with a finality.

Bitter cold wind nipped at his skin. He stood staring at the door for a long time before returning to his car.

He'd done the right thing for her, but he'd never anticipated losing her completely.

CHAPTER EIGHT

By Sunday afternoon, Hunter was ready to tear off any Dragon's head. A sleepless night thinking about Kira, replaying their conversation, replaying their kiss, drove him crazy. When the Blades took to the ice, he powered through his shifts, pushing his body, ignoring its signals to slow down. The chill in the air raised his annoyance up another notch. Single-digit temperatures. Again. And being inside the rink wasn't much better.

Winter was too damn long, and the cold made him too damn slow. Even so, he'd worked damn hard on his speed. He wasn't the fastest guy on the team, but he wasn't the slowest either. Being a defenseman suited him. He likened prohibiting the opposing team from scoring to what he did in his day job, prohibiting hackers from attacking his systems. Damon had the speed to play center and preferred leading the attack. And Aidan found his own Zen minding the net.

He could use a little of Aidan's Zen right now.

Kira sat in the front row, next to their bench.

Alone.

He'd done the right thing. He had to keep reminding himself that he'd done the right thing.

She deserved someone whole. Someone who wouldn't hurt her.

But seeing her there behind the glass hurt *him*. He couldn't have her, no matter how much he wanted her.

Throughout the first two periods, he kept glancing at her. During a timeout late in the second, he sat on the bench next to Damon, strategizing about how to best the Dragons' star player. The Blades were down, two-nothing, and needed to turn things around.

Waverly skated past him, smirking. He stopped right in front of Kira and pounded on the glass. "Hey, sweetie, are you lacing them up today? Your boyfriend needs some help out here. I wouldn't mind seeing you in action, baby. I've been waiting for it all game. Stand up and show me what you've got."

His words echoed around the rink.

Damon growled and stood. "Is he talking to my sister?"

Fury searing his muscles, Hunter jumped over the boards. He sped toward Waverly.

The jerk turned toward him and fucking grinned. "What, I can't talk to your hot girlfriend?"

Hunter raised his gloved fist and moved closer. Too late, he realized Waverly's plan. If he attacked, he'd be tossed from the game. He pivoted his skates. Rather than checking him into the glass, or, better yet, through the glass, he shoved hard at the opposing winger's chest.

The asshole fell to the ice, then scrambled to stand. He pushed against Hunter's shoulder, hard enough to send him back a few feet.

Needing to channel that rage, Hunter advanced. "You wanna go?"

"Let's go."

They dropped their gloves, and the crowd cheered.

Hunter landed a punch to Waverly's jaw. "That's for looking at her."

Then another. "That's for talking to her."

Waverly countered, tugging on his jersey. Hunter's left arm tangled in the sleeve, but he threw a right hook and caught the winger in the eye. Waverly's head snapped back, and he fell to the ice. His hold on the jersey pulled Hunter off balance, and Hunter went down, landing on top of his opponent.

The ref pulled him off of Waverly. "Let's go, boys. You're both in the box."

They both got five minutes for fighting. The ref added two minutes to Hunter's time for instigating. His team would be shorthanded.

He didn't care.

He skated by his bench. His teammates tapped their sticks against the boards in support. No way were they happy about being down a man. But anytime anyone took down Waverly, it was cause for celebration.

The penalty box gave him a great view of the players' bench and of Kira. He focused on the on-ice action and didn't let his gaze drift to her or to Waverly in the adjoining box.

Finally, his time in the sin bin ended. He jumped on the ice and joined the play.

Waverly set up for a slap shot. Hunter twisted his body to help block the shot. His gaze landed on Kira leaving her seat. Where was she going? If Waverly had chased her away…

The puck ricocheted off of his leg. Hunter winced against the sting as it intensified into a pins-and-needles sensation radiating from his thigh through his foot.

Clenching his jaw against the discomfort, he fought back the string of obscenities, determined not to let Waverly see his pain.

Damon skated over, followed by Aidan. "Are you okay?"

"Don't know. Damn, that struck me in just the right spot." He tested putting his full weight on his leg. Nope, not something he could skate through. Sucking in a breath through his teeth, he bore down against the pain. More of his teammates gathered around him. He hated being a spectacle.

"I was watching him. He shifted his stance and shot it right at you." Damon's gaze narrowed. "Don't worry, I'll take care of it."

Other teammates nodded and murmured their intentions to take Waverly down in retaliation.

Aidan jerked his head toward the bench. "You have to sit out for a while. You can't play this way."

"Yeah, yeah. I know." He didn't like missing any

shifts. Chambers was already hopping over the boards to replace him.

Aidan put his arm around Hunter's shoulders. "Let's get you over there."

"I can manage on my own." That was a lie, and his friends obviously knew it.

The goalie didn't let go, but Aidan humored him with his reply, "Even so."

Damon flanked his other side. "Stop being stubborn. Go sit down so I can kick Waverly's ass."

His friends wouldn't be deterred. Hunter allowed them to guide him to the bench, not that he had much choice. He glanced over his shoulder at Waverly, as the opposing winger smirked from his place on the ice. "Make sure to save me a piece."

Mood as black as the puck careening around the ring, he settled onto the end of the bench. Maybe Kira walking away was a good thing. This way, she wouldn't witness his weakness, wouldn't see his brokenness on display, and wouldn't see how his teammates had to fight his battle for him.

Kira tucked her pea coat tighter around her body and huddled on the metal bench. The coffee she'd purchased at the concession stand was bitter and had cooled too quickly. She shouldn't have come to the game. The arena was freezing and loud, and her gaze kept drifting to Hunter.

He'd come to her rescue and had taken out Waverly. But did it mean anything? After he'd left her house the previous evening, she'd licked her wounds by sending Byron a message, inviting him to her brother's hockey game. One last chance at meeting up. But with only ten minutes remaining until the end of the game, she'd marked him down for another no-show. Three chances were plenty patient. She wouldn't be contacting him again or answering any messages if he happened to send them.

She couldn't contact Hunter again either unless something went wrong with her computer at the office. Her gaze fell to his broad shoulders. From his position on the bench, he yelled something to one of the guys on the ice. He hadn't played a shift since taking that hit in the second period. She told herself not to care, but she couldn't stop caring. This no-contact rule was like tearing away something vital from her soul.

"Kira." Grant wove his way through the bleachers. "Hey, how are you?"

She lifted her hand and waved. "What are you doing here?"

"The guys talk so much about their team, I thought it was time I came out and supported them. I've been sitting on the other side of the rink. Didn't see you until now. Great game." He offered her a warm smile and claimed the space at her side. "How was your video chat yesterday?"

She shook her head and turned her attention to the ice. "It wasn't what I expected."

"Good or bad?"

"Not great. I don't want to talk about it." She tucked her hair behind her ears and switched to a safe topic. "How are the kitchen renovations going?"

He'd been talking about his home renovation projects for the past few months. "Fantastic. The contractor just finished the last part this morning. I'm breaking it in tonight."

"What are you planning on cooking?"

"What do you feel like eating?" He slid closer, and his voice lowered and deepened. "I'd love to cook for you. Maybe we could go for a drive afterward. What do you say?"

"I'd say that sounds very much like a date, so you should save that line for one of your Clicked Hearts women." The only person she wanted to have an evening like that with was Hunter. She'd need to start looking for new matches soon. "I have plans with my brother."

She shifted away from Grant and turned her head toward the bench. Her gaze collided with Hunter's. Heat aching, she tore her focus to the action on the ice.

As frustrated as she was with him, a part of her understood his reasoning for not wanting to get involved. Damon had come out of the Army a different person than when he'd gone in. Of the three men, she'd thought Aidan to be affected the most by PTSD, but Aidan had been open to receiving help. Hunter, on the other hand... Sometimes she'd catch him brooding. She'd mentioned dark moods to him yesterday. He'd never talked about his time overseas with her, so she wasn't sure if he suffered the same way as Aidan. She knew about the physical pain, and while Hunter had only snapped at her on occasion, pain could cause tempers to flare or patience to wear thin. And his insistence on not needing help would war with her wanting to help. Maybe they would only end up fighting and hurting each other.

The buzzer sounded, ending the game. The Blades won by a score of four-to-two. Hunter stood and climbed over the boards and congratulated the guys as they gathered in front of the bench. He hugged Damon and Aidan. The trio had been through a lot together. Hunter's words came back to her... *My lifeline.* He needed them. She couldn't blame him for being wary of something that could drive a wedge between him and his support system.

Grant moved closer again. "Is the team going out after the game?"

Damn it. Why was he bothering with her today? She stood and began making her way to the aisle. "Some of the guys are grabbing dinner at O'Malley's."

"Cool. Maybe I'll tag along."

"If you want." She caught Damon's attention. He waved and pointed toward the locker room. She managed to shake Grant loose and then waited for her brother in their prearranged meeting spot, the hallway leading to the players' area. He'd asked her to join the team for dinner, but if Hunter was going to be there, she thought it best that she should stay away.

A short time later, Damon came of out the locker room, hair still damp from his shower. The bag holding his hockey equipment was slung over one shoulder. "Hey, kid. Ready to head to the pub?"

"I think I'll skip it tonight."

"Why?" Aidan joined them. "You always come to O'Malley's with us after a game. You have to come. We're celebrating. Not only the win, but also the shiner Hunter plastered on Waverly, and Waverly getting tossed from the game at the end."

A few more of the guys came through the door. She greeted them and responded to more invites.

Damon swung his arm over her shoulder. "Tag along. I haven't spent any time with you in a while."

He looked tired. He'd probably been pushing himself too hard again. She wanted to hunt Ursula down and scratch her eyes out. No one hurt her family. "Okay, I'll go. If only to buy you a beer for checking that jerk into the boards."

"Waverly? Yeah, he went down so many times, he'll be feeling sore for weeks. But that's what you get when you mess with one of our teammates. And you, of course."

Hunter hadn't come out yet. He was usually one of the last ones anyway, but he had taken that hit, and been involved in that fight. If he needed help... "Where's Hunter?"

Aidan inclined his head toward the locker room. "I'll wait for him. You guys go on ahead and grab us a table."

The pub was close to the arena, and the team had taken over the bar area. Kira settled at a high top table with Damon, listening to his commentary of the game, and a blow-by-blow encounter of how both he and Aidan had tried taking out Waverly after the jerk had hurt Hunter's leg.

Grant joined them, claiming the seat next to her. She listened to more of his renovation descriptions. Hunter and Aidan walked in during his story about choosing between granite and quartz countertops, and Grant's voice was reduced to a buzzing in her ear. Hunter claimed all her attention. Beer in hand, he moved slowly through the crowded space.

Kira glanced around. The team had taken up four tables. None had a free chair. He might need to sit. When he reached their table, she hopped off the high stool. His eyes narrowed. He probably thought she was leaving because he'd arrived. She wouldn't correct his thought, and she didn't want to risk hurting his pride by offering up her chair in front of his teammates. "Well, I'm grabbing another round. Anyone need anything?"

"I'll join you." Grant smiled and followed her to the bar. He stood too close. She moved a step away. She wasn't sure what had gotten into him, but she wanted it to stop. When a blonde woman sitting at the bar complimented Grant's sweater, she made sure the woman knew he was single. All the women he'd talked about from his online dates were blondes.

With Grant out of her hair, she turned to order her drink. The bartender's flirting soothed her hurt feelings.

If Hunter wouldn't let himself be with her, then she needed to move on. She flirted back but felt hollow inside. She wasn't ready.

She also wasn't ready to sit at a table with him. She shouldn't have come.

A large hand touched her shoulder. She glanced to her right. Aidan stood beside her. The tallest and quietest of the three, he always seemed the most intuitive. "You okay?"

Drumming up a smile, she forced false cheer into her voice. "Sure."

"What's going on between you and my boy over there?" He nodded toward Hunter. "You two have a fight?"

"I guess you could say we cleared the air on a few things. It's... complicated." She took a sip of her wine.

He signaled for another beer. "Of course, it is. Nothing worthwhile is ever easy."

That garnered a real smile. "Sounds like you've been reading inspirational quotes again."

"I'm just naturally wise." With a shoulder shrug and a twinkle in his eyes, he raised the fresh beer to his lips. "What happened between you two is your business. I'm not asking for details, but I will say one thing. Don't let whatever this is come between you guys."

Not spending time with Hunter also meant not spending time with Aidan. She'd miss this gentle giant. "It's sort of a rock-and-a-hard-place situation."

"I have another quote for that too: flow like water."

"I'll keep that in mind. Can you do me a favor?"

"Name it."

"I'm taking a break from the morning run group." Even as she said the words, they hurt. This slow distancing was hell. "Can you make sure someone runs with Hunter?"

He nodded. "I always look out for my crew, you included. I take it this break from the group is because of those... complications?"

Moving the wine glass from one hand to the other, she studied the swirling liquid. "My knees have been bothering me. I decided to switch to yoga in the mornings instead of running."

"Hmmm. I think that's the first lie you've ever told me."

"Lie?" She blinked at him. Heat flushed into her cheeks at his no-nonsense, zero-bullshit expression.

Aidan raised a brow. "You took too long to answer, you're fidgeting more than usual, and you couldn't meet my gaze when you told me. Plus, you're blushing."

There wasn't any use in hiding the truth. She could trust Aidan. "Okay, fine. My yoga studio really does have a morning class, you know. I'll switch to that in the mornings and running on the treadmill at home in the evening. Look, I just... I need to hibernate for a while."

"Hibernate sounds like a lot more than skipping the running group."

"It's just easier this way. And before you ask, Damon doesn't know anything, and I'd like to keep it that way. He has enough going on right now. The tension between Hunter and me will only stress him out."

Aidan regarded her for a long moment. "Okay. But if you need anything during this hibernation, you'll let me know."

It hadn't been a question, and they both knew it, but she responded anyway. "I promise." Careful of her wine and his beer, she hugged him.

"Are you coming back to the table?"

"Sure. Just to finish this, and then I'll head out."

They returned to the table. She stuck by Aidan and let herself be drawn into a conversation with some of the players on the team. They entertained her with stories of games she'd missed, each attempting to outdo the other with outrageous and colorful details that made the games seem more like epic battles of mythological gods rather than guys hanging out and playing a game for fun.

She pretended she really was just Damon's sister, along for the night. But pretending Hunter didn't have a hold on her heart was the hardest part of all.

CHAPTER NINE

Three days after the hockey game, Hunter sat in his office, stewing. He balled up another piece of paper and threw it into the trash can. His concentration had been shot to hell.

He hadn't seen or spoken to Kira since the night in the bar. The beginning of the workweek had dragged by without his daily visits to her office. He didn't have a right or reason to see her anymore. But even though he didn't, he couldn't help noticing that Grant had begun visiting her often. Maybe he was helping her with her dating profile, or being a shoulder to cry on.

His hands clenched into fists at the thought. He shoved away from his desk. He needed to find better ways to handle himself than seething.

Kira hadn't shown up at the Monday or Wednesday morning run. Aidan had told the group she'd decided to switch to yoga for a while. He'd looked directly at Hunter when he'd spoken, and Hunter had a feeling his quiet friend knew more than he'd let on. Aidan could keep secrets and respect privacy. He didn't push for more details. Damon didn't seem to know anything about what had happened with Kira, and it was better that way. The last thing he needed was more tension. Regardless, runs weren't as fun without her by his side.

Nothing was.

The ringing of his phone, from one of the inside lines, was a welcome distraction. Until he saw Grant's name on his screen. "Yeah?"

"My system is running much slower than normal. My reports keep timing out."

"I'll come take a look." He ended the call. Maybe that was rude, but he didn't like the guy very much.

Grant's office was a disorganized mess. Piles of papers overflowed on his desk. Stacks of folders sat on the floor. Grant pointed to the computer. "Maybe I need a new one."

"This one's only a year old. It arrived about a week before you did. I'll figure out why it's slow."

One of the interns had slowed the system down the previous week by streaming music and movies while he'd worked. An easy find and an easy fix.

Grant looked at his Rolex. "Will this take long?"

"It might. It might not." He derived some satisfaction from Grant's grimace. "The problem may be a case of too many things running at the same time. But it could be more serious, like you could need a virus scan, maybe a disk cleanup, and a system reboot."

Grant shrugged his shoulders and tucked his phone

into his pocket. "I have the same things open that I always do. I guess I'll grab an early lunch."

"Good idea. Maybe take a long one." Anything to get him out of the way. Hunter hated people hovering while he worked, but Grant irked him more than anyone else. He thought him to be a pompous ass, and that was before he'd latched onto Kira.

As soon as Grant left, Hunter breathed easier. He sat down at the desk and counted five applications running, the company's main system and email, and accounting software. Not enough to slow things down. He clicked on the browser shortcut and a message box popped up. *Browser didn't shut down properly. Click to restore all pages.* "Let's see how many."

Fifteen pages loaded. News, sports, investments, credit card... And Clicked Hearts.

Clicked Hearts, Clicked Hearts, Clicked Hearts, and Clicked Hearts.

Why did he have five tabs of the same page loaded? He clicked on one. Grant's smiling profile picture greeted him. The chat window with Biker_-Girl_01 showed a very not suitable for work conversation. He clicked on the next tab and paused. A different profile name for Grant and a different picture, where he called himself Jerry, a day trader on Wall Street. The same with the next tab where he claimed to be a cowboy named Clete, and the next page where he listed himself as a contractor named Wilson.

Hunter's lip curled in disgust. Grant didn't exactly

match his choir-boy looks. Why pretend to be all these different men?

"Hunter? What are you doing here? Where's Grant?" Kira glided into the room. The sleeves of her red button-down shirt were rolled to her elbows, giving him a glimpse of slim, honey-toned arms. A silver charm bracelet adorned one wrist. Black skirt, black tights, and black boots covered her lower half. Effortlessly sexy.

He swallowed. Did she have to be so beautiful? And that smile. Even when strained around the edges, as it was now, it killed him. "System problems. He's at lunch."

"Oh." She placed a stack of papers into a bin labeled Receipts on the desk. He didn't miss the tremor in her hand. "Well, I'll let you get back to it."

"Wait. How have you been?" He missed her. Two and a half days since she'd ignored him at the bar, three and a half days since she cut him out of her life, and he missed her.

A delicate shoulder lifted as she backed away. "Fine. Busy. I'd better go."

He didn't want to watch her walk away from him again, so he turned back to the computer and clicked on the last Clicked Hearts page... and his heart missed a beat. "What a bastard. What a fucking bastard."

"Excuse me?" Kira stopped in the doorway.

He couldn't believe it, but there it was, right in front of him. What the hell? Rage fought with confusion. Why would Grant do this to Kira?

She was so perfect, such a warm, wonderful, caring person. She radiated light and happiness. She deserved far better than this. He'd throttle Grant and then let the bastard talk. He needed answers.

"Hunter?" Kira's voice broke into his thoughts.

He turned in his chair.

She walked toward the desk. "What's wrong? I've never heard you growl like that before."

He didn't want to tell her. Didn't want to hurt her. Didn't want to be the one who'd break her heart.

But he couldn't lie to her.

Slowly, he stood. Then took one step toward her. "Byron isn't Byron. I found out Real-Life-Romeo's real identity."

CHAPTER TEN

The temperature in Grant's office climbed by several degrees. Kira stared at Hunter and his tight stance, hands flexing into fists, that muscle ticking in his jaw, and his eyes glittering in a way she'd never seen before—anger hot enough to scare even the toughest enemy. "You found him just now?"

He jerked his head toward Grant's computer. "See for yourself. His handle is the same. One of his many handles."

"Grant? That can't be right." Her stomach tightened. It couldn't be true. Maybe he had a similar name. She leaned over the desk and stared at the screen. Real-Life-Romeo. Same handle, same profile picture, same person. What the hell? "Why? Why would he do this?"

"I don't know. But we're going to find out."

She clicked on the chat window. Every conversation she'd ever had with Byron, listed there in black and white. A flood of emotions—embarrassment, hurt, confusion, and anger—swirled together. Her face grew hot. Her stomach rolled with sickness. "I really don't understand why he'd do this."

"Now I know why he didn't want to meet in person or video chat or talk to you on the phone. It would have given him away." Hunter's voice came from close behind her.

"And with every missed connection or message I'd received, Grant would be right there the next day, asking about how things had gone with Byron, and offering sympathy and encouragement. This is messed up. What a prick."

Strong hands closed over her shoulders. Hunter's scent surrounded her. "I'll kick his ass for you."

She didn't know whether to hit something or cry. "This is my problem, not yours. I can handle it."

He drew her into his chest and his arms wrapped around her—solid, strong, and supportive. "Let me help."

Leaning into his warmth soothed the chill in her body. He wanted to help her, but he wouldn't let himself be with her. She took a moment to gather her resolve, then turned in his arms and faced him. "I appreciate all the help and time you've spent on the whole dating protector thing, but you're released from that duty. Your obligation to Damon no longer extends to me."

His hands moved to her hips. "This has nothing to do with Damon."

"We're not supposed to be friends anymore, remember?"

"I can't turn off my feelings."

His words lanced through her heart. "No. You just choose to ignore them."

His fingers tightened their hold. "Kira."

She lightly pressed against his chest until he released her. Then she stepped back. Rubbing her arms didn't relieve the goosebumps dotting her skin. "I don't want to get into discussing you and me again. You made your choice. I made mine. Thank you for sharing the information about Grant." Honing her emotions into determination, she spoke through tight lips. "Now I'm going to get some answers."

He opened his mouth as if to retort, but his phone sounded with an alert.

She strode out of the room, moving fast, pushing her legs until her muscles burned, not slowing down to talk to anyone. Her mind was a maze of questions. She wouldn't crack, wouldn't show emotion. She wouldn't let anyone see anything but the confident, happy woman they relied on to run their marketing program.

The break room was empty, except for Grant. He stood by the coffee pot, typing something into his phone. Maybe a chat message through Clicked Hearts. Too bad she didn't have her phone. She'd love to catch the prick red-handed.

When he turned, a smile spread across his face. "Hey. Any word from Byron today?"

She wasn't sure how to play it. "I've been too busy to goof off online today, but I'm done with him."

"I'm glad." He tucked his phone into his pocket and

moved closer. "How about we grab a bite after work? We can celebrate you moving on. I picked up some great wine. We can enjoy it by my new fireplace. I promise by the end of the night, you won't be thinking about him anymore."

Disgust rose like bile in her throat. "Grant... I know the truth. Why did you set up that fake profile?"

His brows rose and his mouth dropped open. "What are you talking about?"

"I know you're behind Byron's profile. I want to know why you did it. Why pretend to be someone else?"

He grinned and shrugged his shoulders, not showing any regret or remorse. "You needed to see how perfect you and I would be together."

Confusion clouded her brain. "Wait... You're *proud* of this?"

"All those other guys are wrong for you. You needed to give us a chance."

"We agreed we were better off as friends."

A glint entered his eyes as he slipped his phone into his pocket. "No. You agreed. I knew you just needed more time."

"We don't have any chemistry. No sparks. Nothing. You're a nice guy, at least I thought you were before you pulled this fake profile crap, but there's nothing between us and there never will be."

His eyes narrowed. In one swift move, his fingers latched around her wrists, and he backed her against the wall in between the vending machine and the water cooler. His grip tightened as she struggled against him. "I feel something."

"I don't. Now get off me." Along with her shouting, self-defense training kicked in. She swung up her leg to knee him in the groin as hard as she could.

Her knee made contact. He grimaced and cursed and released his hold, and then crumpled forward into her. And then someone yanked him away.

"She said no, asshole." Murder in his eyes, Hunter fired his fist into Grant's face. With a grunt, he fell against the floor. Hunter tugged him up by his collar, punched him again, and then shoved him hard into the opposite wall, with a hand around his throat.

Damon and Aidan sprinted into the room and pulled Hunter off of Grant. His grip was so strong, it took both of them to dislodge his hand from Grant's throat. A few other curious onlookers peered into the room. Damon kept his hand on Hunter's arm while Aidan restrained a gasping, cursing Grant.

Her brother eyed both men, then turned to Hunter. "It's a good thing we were stopping for a coffee break. What the hell's going on?"

Hunter shook out of Damon's hold. "I walked in here to find Grant pressing Kira up against the wall and her fighting to escape."

In a flash, Damon stood before her. "Are you okay?"

She nodded, rubbing her wrist.

He rounded on Grant. "You put your hands on my sister?"

When he cracked his knuckles and rolled his shoulders and took a step in Grant's direction, Kira grabbed his arm. "Don't do it."

His muscles vibrated with tension, but he stayed still. "I won't."

Grant shook his head. "It wasn't like that."

"It was exactly like that." Kira glared at him, daring him to lie.

Aidan held up his hand. "Enough. Guys, you're coming with me to the HR floor. Damon, have your dad meet us."

Hunter moved closer to Aidan and Grant. "What the hell were you pulling with Kira and that fake profile?"

Grant rubbed his neck. "Who are you to look up my personal information?"

"All I did was click on the site you never logged out of on a company computer, asshole."

"I'll sue you. I'll sue this company. It's a hostile work environment."

Glaring at Grant, Damon wrapped his arm around Kira's shoulders. "You realize we have security cameras, right? Including in here. Kira can sue your ass right back."

"Let's go." Aidan hauled Grant out of the room, calling over his shoulder, "Meet me upstairs."

Breathing hard, Hunter met her gaze. "Let me see your wrists."

"They're fine." They ached like hell. She looked at Damon and fought for control of her emotions. "I just want to go home."

"Can't yet, kid." Damon's voice gentled. "We need

to talk to Mom and Dad, and you'll have to talk to Aidan too, so he can document his files. Let's head up to see them now."

As they walked to the elevator, whispers followed them. She bit the inside of her cheek and groaned. "The whole company is going to find out about this."

Damon pulled out his buzzing phone. "Okay, Aidan has Grant in conference room three. That leaves Aidan's office for Hunter. And Kira, Aidan said that Mom and Dad will meet us in Mom's office."

She kept her focus on Hunter's hands for most of the ride. Red skin and swollen knuckles. When she had better control of her emotions, she raised her gaze to his face. Blue eyes filled with pain and anger, he watched her right back. She cleared her throat. "Thank you for what you did down there."

"Like I told you before, if anyone hurts you, they answer to me."

The elevator doors opened to the HR level. Hunter gave them both a nod, then stepped off.

When the doors closed again, Kira sagged against the wall.

"What's going on between the two of you?" Damon's tone was a mixture of curiosity and wariness. "And don't say *nothing*. I'm not blind or stupid."

"I really don't want to talk about it now."

He simply nodded and took hold of her hands to examine her wrists. "Then we'll talk about it later."

The doors opened with a quiet ping to the executive suite. The moment they entered her mom's office, both her parents rushed over to give her a hug. Assuring them she was fine, she sank onto one of the guest chairs by the desk.

Her dad sat beside her. "Princess, what happened?"

Kira gave them a brief summary of what happened in the break room and the online situation that had led up to it.

Her mom's mouth pressed into a firm line. "I knew those self-defense lessons were a good idea. And I'm so glad Hunter was there to help you. Do you want to press charges against Grant?"

"Only if he makes good on his threat to sue Hunter and the company. Otherwise, as long as I don't have to see him again, I'll be okay." She paused. "I don't have to see him again, right?"

"Don't worry, baby. He'll be gone as soon as we speak with him." Her mom patted her shoulder. "We saw the security footage. You don't have any idea how much I want to hurt him for putting his hands on you. I never take pleasure in firing someone, but this time, I'll relish it."

Her dad hugged her again. "After you're finished with Aidan, take the rest of the day off. I want you to get your wrists looked at too. We'll check on you tonight or one of us can go home with you now and keep you company. Whatever you want."

"Thanks. You can stay here. I just want some tea and quiet and to be alone for a while."

After a few more minutes of hugs and reassurances, her parents and Damon left to meet with Hunter and

Grant. Aidan came in for her interview, and Kira went through the whole story a second time.

He photographed her wrists, then laid a gentle finger over the red skin already bruising. "Ice this when you get home, and call if you need anything."

"I will. Thanks." Between her mom and her dad, Damon, and Aidan, she had a full-scale care staff.

"Hunter's worried about you."

She wasn't prepared for that. "Tell him I'm fine."

"You could tell him yourself."

Pressing her lips together, she shook her head. Aidan didn't try to persuade her, he simply hugged her.

Finally, Damon came in. He held her purse and coat. "I'll walk you out."

She kept her head down as they made their way through the building. Once outside, the cold slapped her skin. Gray clouds blocked out the sun. The mood was somber and depressing.

Damon glanced at the building, then back at her. "Look, I need to get back in there. Are you going to be okay?"

"Sure." She sniffed back the tears. She'd held it together, and just needed to hang on for a little bit longer.

"I know you said you wanted to be alone for a while, but maybe that's not the best idea. I'm going to send Hunter home after he's done with talking to Mom and Dad. Call him. He'll hang out with you."

"I'll be fine on my own. Please don't send him to see me."

He studied her for a moment, seemingly oblivious to the icy wind sliding around them. "Are you ready to talk about what's going on between you two yet?"

"No."

"Do I need to kick his ass?"

"He's your best friend."

"And you're my sister. If anyone hurts you, it's my responsibility to take them down."

"I can take care of myself."

"Kid, I know you can, but taking care of you is something I'm proud to do." He hugged her. "I'll come by tonight, all right?"

Overwhelmed with gratitude for him, she hugged her brother tight. "Thanks."

The sky opened in a rush. Lowering her head, she bid him a quick goodbye and climbed into the car grateful the rain dotting her cheeks masked her tears.

CHAPTER ELEVEN

Hunter paced Aidan's office. He needed to release his anger. He desperately wanted to break through the door and rip off Grant's balls then shove them down the bastard's throat. That might start to take the edge off. But no, instead, he was locked in an office so he wouldn't do anything stupid.

Seeing Kira struggling against the smarmy asshole incited a rage like he'd never known before. Not even in the heat of battle. He needed an outlet, preferably a human punching bag. Where was Waverly when he needed him?

The door opened, and he stopped pacing. Kira's parents entered the room. As soon as the door closed, Nadia hugged him. "Thank you for protecting my baby today."

Stan shook his hand. "Look, son. We don't care what Grant is threatening. You were protecting our daughter from an assault. Your job is safe. You have our backing, legal and whatever else you need. You don't have to worry."

The two people he loved like his own parents stood before him, their faces warm and comforting and offering him everything. They treated him like he was their own son. He didn't deserve it. He couldn't risk dragging them or the company they'd worked their lives to build into his drama.

"I think it's best if I resign."

"Now hold on there—"

"I take full responsibility. I don't think he'll back down. He'll sue, and if I stay, I'm jeopardizing not only the company, but you and Damon, Aidan, and," his voice caught in his throat, "Kira. The most important people in my life. I can't let that happen. I'll keep you and your family and the company out of it as much as I can. Maybe he'll just sue me and leave the company alone."

Both his bosses were quiet for a moment. Nadia spoke first. "Don't make any rash decisions in the heat of the moment. This has been an emotional day. Go home. Take the rest of the week off and think things through. Why don't we talk again on Monday? We may have a better idea of where we stand then. But regardless of what happens, you have our full support."

"We consider you family, Hunter." Stan patted him on the shoulder. "If anyone goes after one of our own, we fight it together."

"Thank you both. I appreciate it." How would Stan and Nadia feel if they knew he'd hurt Kira? All the more reason to go.

He said his goodbyes, agreed to talk to them on Monday, and then left them at the elevator. They headed up to the executive suite while he headed down to his floor. He needed to grab his jacket and close down his desk. When he stepped off the elevator, he ran into Damon and Aidan in the hall.

Aidan held out an ice pack. "For your knuckles."

Hunter accepted the pack with a nod. Aidan took care of him just as much as Damon did. "Got a minute? We all need to talk."

His friends nodded, and Aidan led them into an unused meeting room. "What's up?"

"I just resigned."

"You're doing what?" Damon shoved away from the table. "Why?"

"The lawsuit Grant threatened."

"I refuse to accept it. You're needed here. I'm not going to let some… some… asshole hurt my family and screw with my friends."

As he'd expected, Damon paced and raged while Aidan regarded him quietly. When Damon's tirade ended, Hunter spoke again. "I don't know, maybe I should take off. Go back to LA. Stay with my cousin while I figure things out." One of the only family members he hadn't alienated, Liam would welcome him with open arms.

Aidan shook his head. "Running won't solve anything."

Maybe it wouldn't. But staying didn't seem like the smartest plan either.

He back-stepped toward the door, already putting distance between them. "The warm weather would be good for me. I need it. And I with everything that's happened, I think it's best if I'm gone."

"Hunter. Wait." Damon lifted his hand and moved toward him.

"I'm sorry, man." He turned and walked away. He didn't want to be seen as someone who abandoned his friends, but hard as he'd tried not to, he'd managed to hurt them anyway.

The next morning, Hunter's alarm blared at six-thirty. Forcing himself out of bed was torture. His knuckles were sore, and his thighs ached. A glance at the clock confirmed he had fifteen minutes until the scheduled morning run. After all that had happened the day before, he doubted Damon and Aidan would expect him to show up at the trail, but he'd go anyway. He needed to get used to being on his own. If he moved back to California, he wouldn't have his friends with him.

Dressed in layers, he downed some water and gently stretched. Today was an easy day. Five miles. Easy if the weather would climb over twenty degrees.

When he opened his door, Damon and Aidan stood on the other side.

Jaw set, Damon gave him a curt nod. "Glad to see you didn't take off for Cali yet. We have some things to discuss first."

They weren't going to talk him out of it, but he was grateful for such good friends. He locked the door and pocketed the key. "Okay."

Aidan laid a hand on Hunter's shoulder. "Instead of driving to the trail, let's just run around here."

They set off at an easy pace with Hunter in the middle and the guys flanking either side.

Damon cleared his throat. "After we escorted Grant out yesterday, I went through his computer files to see what else he might have been doing when he should have been working. Got nothing, but I checked out the accounting program while I was at it to see what bills needed to be paid. This month's credit card bill was astronomical. That's when I ransacked his desk. All the company credit card bills were hidden in the bottom of a locked drawer. Turns out for the past six months he's been funneling company money into his home renovations. We would have caught it eventually, but if you hadn't reacted the way you did, it could have gone on for months more. We trusted that guy."

Before Hunter could ask any questions, Damon kept going. "I went right over to his place and confronted him. He claims he'd intended to repay the money before we noticed, but I'm not so sure. I'm combing through every bill he's paid and report he's filed since he was hired."

"What an asshole. Stealing from your family." Hunter shook his head. Shocked didn't begin to cover his feelings. His contempt of Grant grew to new heights. "What did your parents say?"

"Yeah, that wasn't a fun conversation... Anyway, he has two weeks to repay the money. And, I told Grant we won't press charges or go after him in court as long as he doesn't sue you or us for what happened yesterday. He agreed. So I'm ignoring your resignation."

Hunter stopped running. With the snap of his fingers, Damon had fixed everything. "Once again, you're saving my ass."

"You always say that." Eyes narrowed in frustration, Damon stopped running too. He poked his index finger into Hunter's chest. "Do you have any idea what I'd be like if you and Aidan weren't here? Or how much having you guys with me helped when we were in that sandbox overseas? Or how much I rely on you now? Especially while I'm dealing with the mess from Ursula. But more important than that, I wouldn't trust just anyone to watch out for my sister."

He grunted at that. "I couldn't watch out for her fast enough yesterday. The bastard had his hands on her." Anger fired through his veins. "Damn legs slowed me down."

"Your quick thinking to follow her is why he didn't get any further than grabbing her wrists," Aidan pointed out. "I know she can defend herself, and her kneeing him really helped, but still, taking down someone that intent can require more than one person. What if he'd somehow blocked her kick? Things could've gotten so much worse."

Rage flared at the image of Kira pressed against that wall. Hunter's hands tightened into fists. "I wish you guys hadn't pulled me off of him so soon. The few punches I got in weren't enough. Every time I think about it, I want to explode."

Aidan's dark eyes kindled with anger. "Me, too. I'm the one who hired him."

"How do you think I feel? She's my sister." Damon picked up a rock and heaved it across a snow-covered field. "But back to the helping each other out thing, I look at it this way, man. We're even. We all saved each other."

Hunter knew his debt could never be paid. "You saved my life. I can't repay that."

"You want to repay me? Make my sister happy." Damon crossed his arms over his chest and the glint in his gaze dared Hunter to argue. "I talked to her last night. Kira said you won't let anything happen between you two."

Hunter picked up his own rock and hurled it like a baseball. "We talked about this before. I don't want to hurt her."

"You have so much pride. It's damn annoying."

Aidan nodded, as wise as a sage. "Letting someone in isn't a weakness."

"Losing my temper when the pain gets crazy bad is

a weakness." He advanced toward Damon. "I'd think you'd be happy I care enough about her that I don't want to hurt her, and appreciate that I don't want to start something that could change her."

"You've already changed her. For the better. If you care about each other as much as I think you do, you'll both work hard to make the relationship work out."

He rubbed his thigh. Running sucked today. "She needs someone whole."

Damon dropped the rock he'd been holding. "Fuck, nobody's whole. I'm not, and I want and deserve a complete life. So, you have bullet holes in you. Yes, you have nerve damage, from fighting like hell for your country. But you're not missing your freaking heart or brain. She needs someone who will back her up and is there for her. That's you."

Hunter stared at him. He'd never seen Damon so worked up.

Fire burning in his eyes, Damon stalked closer. "And while we're talking about it, you refusing help all the time is damn annoying too."

Aidan met Hunter's gaze. "Damon's a little fired up this morning. But I agree. You should let us help you more and stop fighting it so much. Needing help doesn't make you weak. Accepting it makes you strong."

That scored a direct hit.

"Exactly," Damon added.

"We all make accommodations for each other, right?" Aidan bent and scooped up the rock Damon had dropped. He palmed it a few times and then tossed it into the field. "You guys helped me find a place to ride out Fourth of July where I can avoid fireworks. And you go with me to make sure I won't be alone. You've helped me deal when something triggers my PTSD. Does accepting that help make me weak?"

Hunter shook his head. "You're one of the strongest people I know. You both are."

"Then, let us help more. I understand resenting the things that are part of our new normal now. I miss being able to enjoy fireworks. I hate reacting the way I do to noises that startle me. But when each one happens, and you're right there to help, then dealing with it is easier."

Hunter was quiet for a while as Aidan's words sunk in. "You're right. I promise I'll try to be better about accepting help."

Damon clapped him on the back. "Good. Now back to my sister, don't forget, the supposedly perfect guy turned out to be an asshole. You are what she needs. You're who and what she wants."

"I wish somebody wanted me like she wants you," Aidan chimed in. "You've both been unhappy and staying away from each other hasn't helped. Give in to it. You'll make it work."

"I want it, man, I want it so bad. But I'm scared."

"You're good enough for my sister, man. More than good enough." Damon pulled him into a hug. The threat of tears stung Hunter's eyes, and he chuckled a watery laugh when Aidan stepped over and ruffled his hair.

Sniffling, Hunter pulled back and braved a smile.

"Now can we stop this love fest? We still have four and a half miles to run."

Their laughter echoed off the trees. Hunter looked at his best friends and grinned. They loved him enough to slow down for him to catch up, to be there if he fell, and to kick his ass when he needed it. They believed in him. Believed that he could make Kira happy.

He had to find her, grovel, and hope she could forgive him for how badly he'd messed up.

CHAPTER TWELVE

The morning after the incident, Kira took a personal day off from work. She didn't want to face the sympathetic faces, the whispers, or the rumors. Her phone lit up with concerned well-wishers. A few people mentioned the gossip running rampant around the company about Kira and Grant and the fake profiles.

After the tenth call, she dialed her dad's cell. "I can't go back. Do you know how humiliating this is? Everyone knows."

"Everyone thinks what he did was terrible."

"I can't take all the whispers and gossip. I want to work remotely from now on." She had everything she needed at her home office.

"We need to see you here. You're a vital member of the team."

"Dad, I can't. What if people think I'm a gullible idiot because I fell for what he did?"

"Princess, I wouldn't let a gullible idiot run my

marketing department. Take a few days off. Think things over. Your mother and I told Hunter the same thing when he offered to resign."

She sat up straighter and gripped the phone. "Hunter resigning? Why?"

"He didn't want to drag us through a lawsuit."

"But I thought the suit threat was dropped."

"It is now. But it wasn't when I spoke with him yesterday."

"So, Hunter is staying?"

"Of course. He and I had a long talk this morning. He's a good man, that one. Isn't he, Princess?"

"Yes, Dad." After promising to take the weekend to think about things, she ended the call and looked at her calendar.

One day until Valentine's Day.

She'd failed her goal.

Her appetite nonexistent, she took a cup of herbal tea up to her bedroom and settled onto her bed with her laptop. She logged on to Clicked Hearts. Just seeing the vivid blue and pink was enough to bring memories of Grant. And Hunter.

She couldn't stop caring about Hunter, but her heart could only be kicked so many times, and she'd reached her quota.

Love sucked. She was tired, so tired of the searching and the rejection and the disappointment. Her paired-off friends could keep it.

She deleted her profile.

She was done.

By eight o'clock that evening, Kira had made up her mind. She needed time away from everything. Away from Hunter, away from the rumor mill, and away from the memories of Grant and the Clicked Hearts fiasco. She'd stored up a ton of personal days over the years. Enough that she could be gone for weeks. Months, really.

Not running away… It wasn't running away if you planned on coming back.

Fortified by a combination of caffeine, chocolate, and confidence, she drove into the company parking lot. Only a few cars remained. Thankfully, no one from her team.

She beelined for her office, unlocked the door and slipped inside. Then set the box she'd carried in on the floor by her desk. One by one, she set her personal items inside: coffee cup, calendar, hand lotion, the small potted plant she kept by her window, and the extra sweater she kept on the back of her chair.

Drafting out a list of tasks for the week for her assistant took more time than she'd thought. Her team could handle it without her there. She set it on her desk, then took a long moment to study her office.

Her parents would understand. She wasn't quitting, wasn't leaving anyone in a lurch. Aidan could find a temporary replacement for her, and she'd work from home until he got someone. She just needed some time and space to let her heart and her pride heal.

"You keep late hours." Hunter's voice filled the room.

Gasping, she dropped her pen and spun around. His wide shoulders filled the doorway. Eyes darkened and brooding, he stared at her. She raised her hands to her heart. "You scared me. What are you doing here? Your car wasn't in the lot when I arrived."

He nodded toward her computer. "When you logged into the system, it showed up in my system scan. I wanted to talk to you, so here I am."

"Oh." She sat back in her chair, wary of what they had left to say to each other.

He stepped inside the room, then shut the door and locked it. His gaze fell to the box on the floor and then landed on her desk. "What the hell?"

As he moved closer, she pushed her chair further away. "I'm leaving for a while."

"No, you're not." He grasped the arms of her chair, caging her in. His crisp citrus and spice scent filled her lungs. Fire burned in his eyes.

"I can't stay right now, not after all that's happened." She pushed against his chest. "Let go."

To her surprise, he did. But then his hands captured hers and he pulled her to her feet. "All the talk around here today was about what a jerk Grant is and sympathy for you. Everyone wanted to tear into him for hurting you."

"I hate all the attention. It makes me uncomfortable. What if they think I'm too gullible or not capable—"

He laid his finger against her lips for a moment. "No

one thinks anything bad about you. You know, I'm actually glad Grant pulled his scheme."

Humiliation burning heat in her cheeks, she gaped at him. "How can you say that?"

His grip on her hands softened to a caress. "Because it made you and me spend more time together. And it forced my feelings for you to the surface. I can't ever be sorry about that."

Tears thickened her throat, and she couldn't respond.

"Do you have any idea how hard it was to hold back when the chemistry between us is so explosive? How good your lips felt against mine, and how right your body felt in my arms? And then to have to pull away when all I wanted to do was hold tight?"

"But you made the choice to do that."

"I know. And I was wrong. What you said to me yesterday morning in his office, and then what happened in the break room made me face my feelings. On top of that, Damon and Aidan kindly kicked my ass."

Her pulse increased, both at his nearness and his words. "So, what are you saying?"

The intensity in his gaze took her breath away. Hunter gently stroked his thumb over her wrist. "There's a light in you. Some sort of energy you give off. A spark. It's beautiful. I was afraid that if we gave in and I hurt you, I'd dim it forever. But I promise I'll do my best not to. I need that light. I need you. I want to keep the friends part, but I want the more-than-friends part, too. If you'll have me."

She squeezed his hands as her heart filled. "You

have to let me in, and let me help you. You need to come to me. If I rely on you, I want you to rely on me, too."

"I will. I do. Life with me may not be easy, but I promise I'll do my best to make you happy." His gaze darkened. He guided her hand down his chest, over his stomach, and cupped her against his erection. "Do you feel what you do to me?"

Her fingers tightened for a moment and pure power flowed into her as she watched his eyes close. "Hunter."

He groaned and then returned her hand to his chest. His heartbeat increased. "And do you feel how hard and fast this is beating for you?"

"It's echoing mine."

His lips hovered over hers. "I want you. In my bed. In my life. I like being with you."

"Me too," she said before he captured her mouth in an aching kiss. She eagerly gave in to the sweet sensation.

He lifted his head and brought her hands up to his lips. A low growl sounded in his throat as he studied the bruises encircling her wrists. Then he placed kisses on each one.

Kira smiled and linked her arms around his neck. Hunter's hands slid along her back, stopping just above her hips. He crushed her to him and sighed. They held each other for long moments until the shadows shifted in the trees.

"Let me help you put your stuff back." He released

his hold and then dug into the box and set item after item back on her desk.

She walked to the small shredder across the room. "I'll take care of my task list."

When she turned around, he was right there and his arms captured her against his body. His lips swooped down and landed, hard and firm, against hers. His tongue coaxed her lips apart and dipped deep inside to tease hers with wet heat.

Her hands flexed on his chest, then curled into the fabric of his shirt. The kisses deepened and lengthened. Her pulse thrummed, and her heart beat wildly, and her body chanted for more.

With a groan, Hunter slowly eased back, but his fist tightened in her hair. "We need to take this someplace else."

"My place is closer." She cupped his cheek and then brushed his hair off his forehead. "Follow me there?"

"I'd follow you anywhere."

CHAPTER THIRTEEN

Hunter followed Kira to her place. Thankfully, she was going to give him a chance. He wasn't going to blow it. He'd work hard, damn hard, to be the kind of man who was always worthy of her. As soon as they were inside, he drew her against him. "Where were we?"

Her arms slipped up to his chest. "I think I was right about here. And you had a hand tightened in my hair, and the other one was roaming over my back."

"Right." He lowered his head. Her lips met his, soft, wet, and open. He delved in and tasted the rich, dark sweetness of her mouth. Her fingers tangled in his hair, and she nipped his bottom lip. On a low groan, he tugged her tighter against him. Her curves meeting up with the planes of his body felt so freaking good.

Kira slipped her fingers under his sweater, and he sucked in a breath when her nails scraped along his skin. Humming a sound of approval, she skimmed her delicate fingertips higher and higher and then dropped down low to tease the skin at his waistband.

With one hand, he pulled the sweater and underlying shirt over his head.

Her murmur of approval as she studied his body stroked his ego, and with sure hands, she traced his muscles with an appreciation only a fellow athlete could understand.

Being touched felt so good, but he needed to keep up. He cupped her breasts and the weight of them in his hands sparked all sorts of ideas for how to draw the most pleasure. Kira sighed and pressed into him and arched her back in an invitation for him to take more. So he did. He lowered his head and parted the knit of her wrap-sweater, and encountered another barrier—a long-sleeved t-shirt in soft heather gray.

He was firing on all circuits but didn't want to push too far too fast.

Kira solved his problem by pushing off her sweater and pulling off her tee.

"Incredible. You're so beautiful." Curves and toned muscles, and he couldn't wait to explore every inch. "Does us being together mean I get my running buddy back?"

"Yes." Her eyes closed when his hand began to journey from her lower abs, over her stomach, and finally touching the pink lace material covering her breasts. "Should we take this to the bedroom?"

He stopped caressing. Rock hard and desperate to be

connected, he wanted her comfortable more than anything else. "Your call."

"I vote yes. We've been building up to this for at least the last two years. I don't want to rush it, but I also don't want to wait any longer to feel you."

"The last two years? More like four. I knew something was special about you right off." He wasn't feeding her a line. Something about her radiated light and happiness.

Keeping her fingers tucked into his belt loops, she walked them backward until she reached her bedroom. Moonlight cast a soft glow in the darkened room. They paused beside the bed, and she slipped off her bra, boots, jeans, and panties while he ridded himself of his shoes, jeans and boxer briefs.

They came together. Hands and lips roamed, tasting, touching, and tempting with promises for more. The heat of Kira, skin to skin, with him was a fantasy come to life. Hunter worshipped every inch, starting at her lips, then moving down her neck, and then following every stroke and caress of her breasts with a trail of kisses over the silky skin.

He dropped to his knees and roamed his exploration lower. Skating his fingers down her sides, he mouthed a path to her core. Fingers teasing that wet heat, he glanced at her face. She bit her lip and dug her fingers into his shoulders.

"Hunter."

"You like that? Me touching you? Have you thought about me doing this? I have. So many times." He added another finger, heard her breath catch, and kept their gazes connected as he lowered his head and then let his tongue join the action. His cock begged for attention, but he focused everything he had on Kira.

The sounds she made drove him on. He stroked and sucked and teased, intent on driving her over the edge. One of her hands moved to his hair. Her grip tightened as her body bowed and he redoubled his efforts, thrilled that she'd let him in, she'd let him get this close, and that he had an entire night ahead to ensure that he gave her as much pleasure as possible.

Breathless and trembling, Kira released her hold on his hair. Hunter gripped the mattress with one hand as he pushed to standing. He tried to hide his grimace at the tingling pain, but Kira must have caught it because she cupped his face in her hands and kissed him. "All right?"

He remembered his promise to let her in. "Yeah. I'm in a bit of pain. But I don't want anything to get in the way of tonight."

She turned on the bedside lamp. "Nothing's going to stop tonight, Hunter. I promise. Let's get more comfortable."

"Kira." Hunter reached for her and kissed her, slow and deep.

With a smile, she took his hand and drew him with her onto the bed. "Lie back and let me take care of you."

She knelt between his legs. Her fingers traced over his stomach, then the muscles in his calves and thighs, then his cock, light at first, then firmer, surer strokes, turning his body into a giant mass of sensations.

He couldn't keep his hands still—touching her hair, her shoulders, her face. She was soft everywhere, like silk.

"There's something I've wanted to do for a long time. Years, actually." Her eyes swam with emotion. Keeping her gaze on his, she scooted back and lowered her head. She bypassed his aching cock and headed for his thighs. Soft lips pressed gentle kisses to the puck-ered scars in his skin. Each mark was a reminder of the hell he'd endured, but now, whenever he'd look down at them, he'd remember Kira and the way she'd kissed them better.

He swallowed hard against the lump forming in his throat. She was incredible, amazing, and everything he needed.

When she glanced up and smiled, he knew he'd lost his heart to her forever.

"Come here." He pulled her up until she laid stretched out along his side. He cupped her face in his hand and stared into the warm brown gaze and beautiful smile that he wanted to see in his bed every morning for the rest of his life. "I love you."

"I love you, too. I have for years." Her body snug-gled into his, creating a subtle friction that drove him crazy.

He worked his hand between them and soon she was rocking into his fingers, drawing closer to the edge. Hunter's eyes closed as her hand wrapped around his cock. She stroked him in a tight grip, and her thumb teased the head in a way that made his eyes roll back and pleasure well to overflowing.

"Too damn good, if you keep that up, I won't last. And I want the first time I come with you to be inside you."

Eyes misted with passion gazed at him. She raised a brow and teased the head of his cock again. "I want to make you feel good, but I want you inside me too."

The words alone almost made him lose control. "I want you to come for me first." His voice rasped the words. "Let me see you come undone, lose control one more time. Then I can sink into you. The way you're gripping my fingers right now, imagine it's my cock. Imagine coming on my cock. I can't wait to feel that."

"Me neither." Kira's breathy whisper teased his lips. And then she kissed him, and he slipped his tongue inside and mimicked the motion of his fingers.

Caught up in the way Kira's lips parted and the soft pants that accompanied the pleasure washing over her features, Hunter thrusted his cock against her hip. As she crested over, clinging to him, he nearly came. Getting her off pretty much got him off. She was stunning.

He nipped her lips. "I need to be inside you."

Kira reached into her bedside table and withdrew a condom. With a breathless kiss, she pushed Hunter's hand away and opened the foil square, and then rolled the latex down his length. He couldn't help flexing his hips into her tight grasp.

She scissored her smooth legs between his thighs. He lifted her leg higher over his hip, and paused, throbbing, at her entrance. With a sexy smile, she angled her hips. "Come inside."

He thrust forward and filled her. Overwhelmed by the tight heat, he groaned. The position pulled him deep inside her. It also took all of the pressure and tension off of his aching thighs, not that he'd let anything—including nerve pain—stop him from being with Kira like this.

Her breath caught. She gripped his hair, holding tight while her body adjusted to his size. He paused to kiss her slow and deep, stroking her arm with his fingers.

With a low moan, she returned the kiss. They began circling their hips in a slow grind. Her hand reached behind him and she raked her nails lightly along his back. Electric shivers zinged along his spine, and he moaned in approval.

He kept kissing her, rocking faster, harder, spurred on by her undulating hips and gasps of his name. Kira in the heat of passion was a goddess and he would happily worship her the rest of his days.

Pleasure swelled and Hunter felt the tell-tale tingling at the base of his spine. He held back, grasping the last thread of control until Kira clutched him and cried out her release, and then he followed her over the edge into ecstasy.

Breathing hard, he held on, damp palms skimming up her back, as his system slowly recovered. "Wow."

"You can say that again." Kira smiled at him. She drew her fingers through his hair in a lazy pattern.

"Okay. Wow." He grinned and leaned in. He had to kiss her again.

Soft lips, tasting of salt and the sweetness that was Kira, met his own. When she pulled away, she caressed his face. "I didn't think we'd ever get here."

"There's no place else I want to be." Brushing his hand over the curve of her hip, he guided her closer once more.

"Can you stay the night?" A faint blush crept into her cheeks. "I really want to fall asleep with you and wake up with you on Valentine's Day. Not that we have to do anything special tomorrow. I know a lot of people feel pressured about the holiday, and I don't want—"

He cut off the flow of words with a quick kiss. "You deserve all the romance in the world. And I'm going to make sure you get it. Starting now."

She glided her foot up the back of his leg and locked him in tight. "I like the sound of that."

His body came alive again, swirling with sensations as she clamped around him and he hardened inside her. "Me too. So I better get started."

CHAPTER FOURTEEN

Kira sat at her desk, counting down the minutes until five o'clock, smiling at the reminders of the holiday littering her desk. The red heart adorning her to-go cup of coffee, the heart-shaped cookie Hunter had swiped from the break room for her, a Valentine from Emily all the way from France, and the little bag of conversation hearts her parents had placed on every employee's desk. She definitely felt the love.

Hunter had woken her that morning, suggesting they return to the Greek restaurant, the scene of their first date, for their first Valentine's Day dinner together. He'd called Athena, and had even managed to get their same table. She couldn't wait.

They'd missed the morning run with the group, opting to spend the extra hour in bed, indulging in slow, steamy sex that got her heartbeat pounding as much as a wind sprint.

"Hey, kid." Damon's voice jarred her out of her reverie.

She glanced at the doorway. Damon stood in the middle, flanked by Hunter and Aidan. All three grinned at her.

"What's up?"

"We thought we'd accompany Hunter down to visit."

Hunter pushed past them. He set a file on her desk and then came around to her chair. She smiled up at him. That he was really there and they were really together, overwhelmed her. Holding onto the arms of the chair, he leaned down and kissed her. The combination of firm lips and a slow, soft kiss dissolved her thoughts. He'd kept the kiss light, but she felt it all the way down to her toes.

Damon clapped his hands together twice. "Okay, okay. Enough. I'm happy for you guys, but she's still my sister."

Leaning on Hunter, she wrapped her arms around his waist and then turned her head toward her brother. "It's your fault, you know. Asking him to keep an eye on me."

A full grin broke out on Damon's face. So rare these days. "I take full credit."

After a few more minutes of chatting, Damon and Aidan left.

The clock on the wall across from her desk struck five o'clock. Kira eased out of Hunter's embrace.

"Ready to go? Our reservations are for six o'clock, right?"

"Yeah. Hey, I was thinking, how about packing a bag and we hang out at my place this weekend?"

As he'd promised, he was letting her in. "Sure. If we leave now, we'll have time to stop by my place so I can pack that bag before dinner, then after we eat, we can head straight home to your house." She had a sexy, little red ensemble that she planned to slip into after dinner. Her Valentine to him.

"Don't forget running clothes." He smiled and stood. "I'm looking forward to getting my running buddy back."

"Me too. So, let's go."

"One thing first." He strode to her door, closed it, and locked it.

She placed her hands on her hips. "What are you doing?"

He rounded the desk. "Getting ready to kiss you properly. That kiss with the guys in the room didn't count, and I don't want to have to wait until we get to the car."

"Hey, I'm not complaining." She slipped her arms around his neck. "I'll always have time to kiss you."

"Good." He leaned down and hooked his arm around her back, and his other around her waist.

Caught close against him, she studied the face she loved. Her fingertips traveled over strong bones, his straight nose, sweeping brows, and that firm mouth. She cupped her hand on his jaw. "Kiss me?"

"Always." In classic movie kiss mode, he crushed his mouth to hers and then suddenly the room was moving. No, she was moving. Her arms clung to his neck and her eyes fluttered open. He'd *dipped* her.

He smiled down at her, and his warm breath fluttered over her cheek. "You're the most beautiful woman I've ever known. Not just your looks, but your heart."

Her heart beat faster, spurred on by joy like she'd never known. "It belongs to you."

"Well, that's good. Because I have a very important question for you."

"What is it?"

He brought her back to the upright position, then turned away from her and grabbed the file folder from her desk. The folder fluttered to the floor as Hunter turned toward her. He held out a large paper heart cut out of red construction paper. Happiness glittered in his eyes. "Will you be my valentine?"

A huge grin spread across her face. She reached out to trace her finger over their names inked on the paper. Love welled inside her, and her heart filled to bursting. "Yes. Definitely yes."

Hunter held one side of the valentine, while she held the other. He linked their other hands together. "I love you."

She tightened her hold. She'd never let go. "I love you, too."

"Good." He smiled and pulled her into his arms. "Now, kiss me again."

EPILOGUE

Hunter turned his car off the main road and followed the
directions Damon had given him the day before. The
city gave way to a large park, thick with flowering trees.
He smiled at seeing spring in full-blast, after a winter
that had seemed to linger on forever.

Beside him, Kira twisted to look out the window.
"Damon said he found a running trail back here?"

"Yeah. Just a little further up."

They drove to the top of a hill. He parked and wiped
damp palms on his running shorts. His heart beat faster.
For weeks, months really, he'd thought about the best
way to propose. And every time, he circled back to the
first thing that had been theirs. She'd been his running
partner, had stayed by his side, slowed her pace to
match his, for months, years, before they'd ever been
anything more than friends.

Feeling for the ring in his pocket, he climbed from
the car. A morning run without Damon and Aidan felt

odd, but his friends knew his plans. They'd gone with him to help pick out the ring and listened to his proposal ideas, even though they'd done more kidding around than actual helping. They were probably three miles into their workout by now, judging by the good luck and congrats texts he'd received earlier. No doubt, they'd check in soon to see how things went with the asking.

Warm sunshine kissed his skin. Hunter lifted his face to the sky and breathed in deep. A field of daffodils spread out below. This was it—the perfect spot.

Kira pushed her sunglasses back and smiled. "It's pretty here. I was surprised the guys canceled today, but I'm glad too. It hasn't been just you and me on a run in a long time. Maybe it's silly to feel that way, given all the time we've been spending together lately."

Lately, they'd been sharing space, staying at each other's places more often than not. He didn't want the day to end without seeing her, and waking up with Kira was way better than waking up alone. He wanted her with him full-time. She seemed to feel the same.

She bent in a graceful, gentle stretch. He couldn't resist grabbing hold of her hips and drawing her against him.

Laughing, she rose and turned in his arms and wrapped her own around him. "Careful. This is a public place. We'd better not start something we can't finish here."

"Can't help myself around you." Holding her close, he stroked his hands down her back.

Her eyes softened. "Me either. But don't lose that thought. We'll pick it up during our post-run massages."

The massages were the best part of a run. Kira would rub his thighs, helping to ease the ache there, but her hands on him were enough to spark a different type of ache—every time. And he was only too happy to return the favor. Those aches, that desperate passion, that need for each other, never faded, no matter how often they fed the desire. Every time they fed it, it grew.

Keeping one hand on her hip, he took one step back. "I love you."

"I love you, too."

In his pocket, his fingers closed around the ring. "And I love what we have. But it's not enough. I need more."

A tiny line formed on her forehead and she moved her arms from his torso to his shoulders. "Okay?"

"You've been my running partner almost since the beginning. And you're on my mind every minute of the day. But I want to create a life with you, make a family together."

Her eyes widened, and her grip on his shoulders increased. "Hunter…"

He pulled out the ring. A heart-shaped stone for his forever Valentine. "I want to make official what's been real in my heart. Will you marry me?"

Tears sparkled in her eyes. Her gaze flashed from his to the ring, then back again. And then she kissed him —long and hard, and the tears on her cheeks spread to his face. His eyes tingled in response. She pulled back with a watery laugh. "I was going to propose to you tonight. You beat me to it."

She was? Pleasure pulsed through him. He reached for her left hand. "So that's a yes?"

"Of course, it's a yes." She watched as he slid the ring home. The smile on her face matched the happiness bursting in his soul.

He leaned in for another kiss. "You still can tonight, if you want to."

"I'll take every chance I get to tell you how you mean the world to me, and how I want only you, and how every time we kiss, I feel like my soul is complete." Kira linked their fingers together. Her ring caught the sunlight, and the diamond's facets burst into a rainbow of colors.

Her words gave him the biggest high he'd ever known. She made him whole. "Maybe we should skip the run and head home. We can pretend it's tonight now."

"It might take from now to tonight to really show you how much I love you." She drew him to her for a kiss. "I'll start here and then work my way down. Inch by inch."

He fisted his car keys. "Let's go home."

"You have the best ideas." Smiling, Kira hugged him tight. "I've been thinking about asking you for such a long time. I'm not surprised we picked the same day. After all, you're the other half of my heart."

As she was to him.

Holding her hand, he walked toward the car, spotlighted by sunlight, and surrounded by the warm glow of love.

Thank you so much for reading Kiss Me Again! I would appreciate it if you would help others enjoy this book too! Please recommend to others and leave a review. Reviews, even if one-line long, help other readers to find authors' books.

Want more Holiday stories? Check out what's next in the Holiday Hearts NY series:

More Than Words

Aidan MacKay may be cool, calm, and collected in his Human Resources position for his Army buddy's toy company, but his battle with PTSD is anything but easy. Things change when he hires voiceover artist Skye Galen to record several company projects. Her voice calm, soothing, and just what Aidan needs. Their exchanges through email and phone calls only make him want more.

Skye has her own demons. After being burned in a fire, she's become a near-recluse. Hiding from the world is easier than facing people's reactions. She is intrigued by Aidan and yearns for more but doesn't believe he can see past her scars.

Aidan is determined to meet the woman behind the voice. Skye knows she'll have to brave the meeting if she wants her lucrative contract with his company to continue.

Sparks fly, and they begin a tentative relationship. But Aidan fears his PTSD may scare Skye away. And Skye worries her insecurities will eventually push Aidan away.

As the fourth of July draws near, fireworks are a guarantee, but they'll both have to face their biggest fears if they don't want their love to implode.

Thank you so much for reading *More Than Words*! If you liked it, please leave a review. Reviews help other readers find my books.

All I Want

Damon Kallis is always in control, whether in his VP position for his family's toy company, captaining his men's rec league hockey team, or taking care of his friends. There isn't any room for romance in his well-ordered life. He made that mistake once, and it nearly cost him everything. Work, family, and friends are all he needs.

All Emily Lombardi needs is a job. After her ex poisoned her reputation as a reporter, no TV station is willing to give her a chance. When the job as Damon's executive assistant opens up, she's in the right place at the right time. Landing the position is simple compared to dealing with Damon -- the stubborn man won't let her in.

Working in close quarters leads to accidental touches, lingering glances, and simmering passion. Soon, they can't deny their attraction.

With the holiday season under way, Damon's ice starts to thaw, and Emily sees someone caring and real, someone she could count on. But their past experiences are hard to forget, and when their new-found love is tested, only a Christmas miracle can give them a happily-ever-after.

Marry Me

Join Kira and Hunter from Kiss Me Again, Aidan and Skye from More Than Words, and Emily and Damon from All I Want as they say their I do's.

Kira and Hunter have been planning their wedding for months. When their venue goes up in smoke two months before their big day, they are left scrambling to find a new location.

Engaged for four months, Skye and Aidan have held off on making wedding plans. Aidan fears that Skye is getting cold feet, but Skye's reluctance stems from her mother's overbearing behavior. Still, she can't put off the wedding forever. She just wants a way to celebrate without the focus being so much on herself.

And newly-engaged Damon can't wait to marry Emily, but her family is insisting on a wedding venue that's booked solid for the next three years. He's not happy about waiting but doesn't see a way around it. Emily longs for something more unique and personal but is afraid to hurt the family by breaking with tradition.

When Emily recommends her favorite vacation spot as a substitute venue for Kira and Hunter, moving the wedding from Holiday, NY to Virginia Beach, VA, Damon sees an opportunity to solve all three couples' problems—a triple wedding.

But a March nor'easter bearing down on the East Coast the weekend of their wedding spells disaster for the couples. And that's only the beginning.

Find all the Holiday Hearts series books here:
https://www.susanscottshelley.com/holidayhearts

ABOUT THE AUTHOR

USA TODAY bestselling author Susan Scott Shelley writes romance with heat and heart that celebrates love without limits. She enjoys watching hockey, training for her next run, reading romance novels, and binging episodes of her favorite British TV shows. Susan lives in Philadelphia with her husband and also works as a professional voice over artist. A city girl who likes being out in nature as often as possible, she has yet to meet a plant she hasn't wanted to take home and she really wants a pet crow.

Visit her website: https://susanscottshelley.com

ALSO BY SUSAN SCOTT SHELLEY

Rekindled, Captivated, Enamored, Game of Love (series box set)

Holiday Hearts series

Kiss Me Again, More Than Words, All I Want, Marry Me, Holiday Hearts (series box set)

Rocked by Love series

Love Notes, Love Song

The Philadelphia Frenzy series

Mad Scramble, Hometown Hero, Team Spirit

Bliss Bakery series

Sugar Crush, Heart of the Batter

The Falling series

Falling Faster

Other Novellas

Simmering Ice, Flirting on Ice, Iced (series box set)

Tackled by the Girl Next Door